Murder Down In Carthage

Cliff Robison

Rock and Fire Press
Salinas, CA

Murder Down In Carthage
© 2024 by Cliff Robison

Library of Congress Catalog Number:

ISBN-13:
978-1-949005-26-4 (print)
978-1-949005-27-1 (eBook)
FIRST EDITION
First Printing

Rock and Fire Press
Salinas, CA

This story is a work of fiction. All Characters
Are figments of my imagination.

DISCLAIMER:

This is a work of fiction.
All of the persons and events described, and most of the places,
are figments of the author's imagination. Any resemblance
to real persons and real events is purely coincidental.

N*I*A*C*IN denies any involvement.

Murder Down in Carthage
Chapter One

There's a party down in Carthage,
In the old town Punic square;
And all the peeps who don't believe,
You know they'll all be there.

THE TRAIN WAS RUNNING late. There had been an interminable delay in leaving Salinas – apparently there had been some sort of drama going on in the business class car – but now the darkness was rolling smoothly past the windows. A string of lights off to his left – to the west, he supposed – marked the US 101 highway. At some point soon, probably near Gilroy, he guessed that the freeway would be harder to spot, but for the moment, it ran nearly parallel.

It was kind of restful, sitting in the soft seat, letting the darkness slide past. He was tempted to shirk his responsibilities, and to just enjoy the ride. He could skip outlining the speech, and just speak extemporaneously. Depending on the evening's main theme – and he hoped that he would be able to discern a main theme of some kind – He could make up a response and steer his speech accordingly.

The car swayed gently side to side, as if to shake him from his stupor. It wouldn't be right, to promise a keynote speech and to deliver a rehash of Sunday's sermon. He needed to be able to offer something that was made to order for the situation.

Jake reached up and clicked on the small lamp overhead, putting a tiny spot of light on his lap, somewhat adjacent to his tray table. In the dimness it offered, he could make out his own writing on the steno pad, but not very well. The pamphlet from the OAR lay beside it, also somewhat obscured.

On reflection, he supposed that a trip to the observation car might be more comfortable for writing a speech. It would provide better lighting and tables on which to write. And it would allow him to procrastinate a few minutes longer.

Plus, he could do with a cup of coffee. It was probably his imagination, but the coach car was feeling a bit cold and drafty. It hadn't felt that way a moment ago, but it certainly did now.

He turned off the dim overhead light and stood up, rocking slightly with the moving train. It reminded him of his time aboard ships, and his old sea legs were quickly coming back to him, allowing him to walk fairly quickly along the car. He set his feet as far apart as the aisle allowed, keeping him stable side to side, and he leaned forward, allowing his momentum to pull him onward. He kept a weather eye for people standing up, or for any obstacles, but there were none, and he moved through the darkened car with ease.

The next car forward was also a coach car, and then there was a business class car. Business class looked much like coach, except that it had leather seats and was less full. He couldn't help noticing one large middle-aged lady, covered by a plush purple coat and wearing a furry purple hat that reminded him of an old Soviet Premier. She turned her head and scowled at him as he passed by.

As he passed through the coupling to the next car, he had a sudden vision of Leonid Brezhnev wearing that purple hat. This was replaced by Nikita Khrushchev, wearing the hat while beating his shoe on a podium. Jake choked trying not to laugh out loud, coughed twice, and kept on going forward.

The observation car was mostly empty, since the darkness offered little to observe. For the most part, the large windows simply reflected back into the car, like so many mirrors. Still, the car was nicely apportioned, and brightly lit, which made it a much better place for writing his speech. Among its many other advantages, it had many tables.

He made his way down the narrow steps to the snack bar, and moments later, returned carrying a cup of coffee. He arrayed the coffee, a ball-point pen, and his steno pad on the table of one of the café-style booths at one end of the car.

He sipped the coffee and glanced at the steno pad. He sighed. Thus far, all that he had written was, "I would like to thank the OAR for graciously inviting me to come and to speak the keynote address."

Below that, the steno page was blank. He murmured the sentence aloud, in hopes that it would flow into another phrase, and then another, until he established a bit of momentum. It did not do so. Reaching the end of the sentence was like slamming his mind against a brick wall.

It wasn't normally this difficult. His sermons often wrote themselves: A passage of scripture, exposition on that scripture, an illustration, often drawn from something that had happened to him that week, and a few parallel verses to support it.

Well, sometimes. Other times, he would spend hours in a commentary to really find the meat of a verse, and would go down a rabbit hole of meanings and parallels. Once, long ago, he had lost track of time, studied all night, and the following morning had been almost unable to put words in the right order. One of the elderly men of the church had complimented that sermon, leading him to suspect that the man had slept through it entirely.

He took another sip of the hot, sweet, and somewhat decent coffee. It was much better than he had feared. He had expected something akin to the horrible brew that the navy had taught him to swill, so finding it potable and pleasant was a nice surprise. Now, back to writing the keynote address.

Various inanities came to mind, mostly rambling run-on sentences about how nice it was to be there. Perhaps the speech should start with a joke; that always seemed to get things rolling. Unfortunately, the first jokes that popped into his mind were from his days as a sailor, and he would rather have died than to say any of them out loud. He had been trying to forget them for close to a decade.

He supposed that it would be easier to write an address if he knew something about the organization. He hadn't heard of them at all until three days prior, when Father Somers, over at St. Paul's Episcopalian, had begged him to fill in. No one else, Somers claimed, could possibly serve.

The nature of the emergency that prompted Somers to cancel was not entirely clear, but he assured Jake that it would be the greatest of all favors if Jake could take this one tiny task off of his hands. It seemed like a small thing – a mere two nights away from home, midweek, on an old island estate in the San Francisco Bay, all expenses paid, with gourmet meals and the freedom to roam the gardens between sessions.

He surmised, from Father Somers' remarks, that the OAR had a vaguely religious purpose, so he might possibly begin with the joke about the priest, minister, and rabbit that had all walked into a blood bank. But surely everyone had heard that one by now. Also, until he knew more about their doctrinal leanings, it might be best to avoid any humor.

He flipped open the brochure and began to read from it. The Organization was founded in 1911, it seems, by an amateur mathematician and admirer of Bertrand Russell. The brochure waxed poetic about the man and about his lofty vision for the future, which this organization would surely bring about, in time, without ever actually spelling out the exact nature of the vision itself.

Jake quickly found himself looking out the window, into the passing darkness. The observation car was well-lit, and the large windows mainly showed him a reflection of himself, but passing lights of a building here, or an intersection there, sometimes showed through the reflection. It made him think of an old stage illusion that relied on reflections, known to photographers as Pepper's ghost.

Still, he primarily just saw himself, procrastinating. He thought about speeches allegedly written on trains, and how some historians have claimed that Lincoln wrote the Gettysburg Address on the back of an envelope while riding a train to the battlefield, but that view was generally dismissed as legend.

And thinking of Lincoln was getting him no closer to having his keynote speech written. He drew a deep breath, took another sip of coffee, and looked back down at the brochure and the nearly blank page on the table.

A grant by the Jeremy Bentham Perpetual Auto-Icon Foundation was received by the Organization in 1931, he read, *and led to the relocation from Chicago to the present location on the west coast.*

Jake vaguely remembered something Dr. Rogers had said about Bentham and his auto-icon. There was something to do with him being, "Present, but not voting." Not that that fact helped at all.

"Reading up on the OAR?" asked a friendly voice, slightly gruff, but cheerful nonetheless. "I couldn't help noticing the brochure. Are you one of us?"

"Not a member," said Jake, as a tallish man with a walrus mustache slid into the seat opposite. "But I'm going to speak at the keynote address."

"Somers? A pleasure to meet you. But I'd expected more of an English accent."

"No, Father Somers had to cancel. He asked me to step in, and cleared it with the organizers. My name is Jake Jacobs."

"Hmmm. Would you happen to be SOJ?"

"No, more SBC. What gave me away as a pastor?"

"The keynote speakers are always ministers of some stripe. It's a curious ironic touch." There was a twinkle in his eye that made Jake wonder what he was walking into.

"You say that as if some sport were involved."

"Well, one mustn't take any of this too seriously. For the most part, it's an excuse to escape the college for a few days. My name is Rodel Dobrazamery. My students call me Dr. D, and my friends call me Rod. So do my patients. As I hope you will."

"Rod, it's nice to meet you. Please call me Jake. I'm afraid I'm at a slight disadvantage, though. To be frank, I'd never even heard of the OAR until Somers asked me to help out."

Dr. D. leaned forward. "*Roma Delenda Est,*" he said.

"I'm a bit rusty in my Roman history, but I think Cato used to say that it was Carthage that must be destroyed."

"Well, those of us in Carthage naturally take the opposite side of that question, as you can imagine." He laughed. "*There's a party down in Carthage, in the old town Punic square; and all the peeps who don't believe, you know they'll all be there.*"

A lady at one of the other tables, some distance from the pair, looked at Dr. D. and recited another line: "*They'll party through the evening, till dawn is in the air; and in the morning wake again…* As I live and breathe! You're Jake Jacobs. Fancy that."

"I am," he said. Her face looked familiar, but it was not until she picked up her bottle of spring water and started to walk towards them that it clicked in his mind. "And you're … Lisa Bertrand? From Cabot?"

"Cabot, El Paso, Searcy – we moved around a bit. But that name is now dead to me. I am now Illuminata." Dobrezamery slid over to give her room, and she perched beside him. She wore matching bracelets, each with a small stone depending from it. One stone was bright green; the other was a translucent shade of pink, so pale in hue that it was nearly white. The bracelets were similar in style, if not in stone, to the moonstone pendant that hung from around her neck, resting on a thick sweater. Over the sweater, she wore a blue vest. "Illuminata McMurray, Doctor of Religious Anthropology."

She was somewhat pretty, though not the way that Jake remembered her, when they both were half as old. She looked sharp and professional; the sort of person who goes to a fashion store knowing beforehand what look she wishes to achieve. At the same time, she gave an academic air, faintly suggesting that what she knew was far more important than how she looked. Sunglasses with huge lenses, in a translucent pink frame, were pushed up on her head, resting in her hair.

"It's a wonder to see you again, Lis- That is, Illuminata." The new name struck Jake as slightly pretentious, which was not how he remembered Lisa. It literally meant, "The enlightened." He tried not to react to it.

"I chose the name when I came to see the truth. So long I lived in the dark, reasoning blindly, by rote. At last I came out of the cave. My eyes were opened to things that others before me knew so very well.

"So I chose my new name. My then-husband suggested it, and it's one of the few things of his that I kept. And his last name; I like it better than Bertrand. Everyone used to put the accent on the second syllable. Drove me nuts.

"And, of course, I raise our daughter. She's fourteen now. We called her Ima Gine, after John Lennon."

It took Jake a moment to connect the sound Emma Jean with John Lennon, but then it clicked. The song, "Imagine." Of course. Subtle, but effective.

"I married three years ago," said Jake. "We're expecting our first. That's why my wife couldn't come along. It's too bad. I'm sure Bryly would have enjoyed meeting you."

"You two are acquainted," said Dr. D. "I would have never imagined. It is so very small of a planet. So very small, indeed. From where exactly do you know each other?"

"We both attended Cabot High School, in Arkansas," said Jake. "We even dated briefly."

"I don't consider that dating, really. We went to one dance, and we were in a few clubs together. Drama, Yearbook, and…"

"Physics club?"

"As if. Sorry, no. But pottery maybe?"

"No, it was chess," he said. "You were known for finding new ways to rook the unwary."

"And you had a way of using knights in pairs. Yes, that was it. The chess club. I wonder what became of Mr. Halberd?"

"I suppose that somewhere, he's still teaching kids how the fianchetto works." Jake smiled at the thought. "Going back for the 15 year reunion this spring?"

"Life has spun me too far," she said. "I can't go back and be that little girl anymore." She shook her head and made a momentary moue.

"Was it William Shakespeare who said, 'Conscience doth make cowards of us all?' Or was that Ben Jonson?" asked Dr. Dobrazamery. "I can never recall."

"I think it's from Hamlet," said Illuminata.

"I believe you're right," said Jake. "I've always suspected that he was also using it to say that knowledge and bravery are opposite attributes. The more we have of the one, the less we have of the other."

"I wouldn't say that you're wrong," said Nata.

"A kind of Heisenberg uncertainty of courage," mused Rod. "Food for thought, at the very least. I suppose that I'll need to read Hamlet again, to see if I can support that."

There was silence for a moment.

"Say, since you're both members of OAR," asked Jake. "Or so it appears – or at the very least, you both know the fight song – is there any chance you can give me some pointers on my keynote address? Things to add, things to leave out?"

"Oh, Jake, you're the keynote speaker?" She said it with a mournful tone, as if she were about to lose a friend. "You don't know, do you?" She shook her head and pointed at the logo on the back of the brochure.

Jake read the name, and it became clear why Father Somers had found a reason to avoid the keynote speech.

Organization of Atheist Researchers.

Chapter Two

"ALL ROADS LEAD TO Rome, or else to Carthage," said Dr. Dobrazamery. "Hence my remark in Latin earlier, that Rome must be destroyed."

"You may be twenty-two centuries too late," replied Jake, as the small boat puttered across the bay. "Rome pretty much closed that door in the second century BC."

It was a little wooden excursion boat, made, no doubt, for sightseeing trips. It was painted white, with bright red and green trim, none of which was visible in the dark that surrounded them. Deep chips and missing splinters, along with what appeared to be carved graffiti, had been painted over here and there, with a color that was not quite the same as the original.

Jake was neither a carpenter nor a boatwright, but it seemed to him that a couple of men could build a boat like this one out of hardware-store lumber in less than a day, and it would not have surprised him if that had been the origin of this boat. Still, it was afloat, moving across the water, and showed no signs of collapse, or at least, not as yet.

He sat on a hard wooden bench, with Illuminata to his left and Dr. D. to his right. He could barely see either of them in the very faint glow that came from miniscule window of the wheelhouse. Around them swirled a foggy haze, making it impossible to pick out any of the lights of the cities across the bay. He idly wondered if the pilot would be able to find the island, or if they'd just keep going until the boat grounded itself somewhere by Mare Island.

"Rome doesn't literally mean Rome, of course. I could have said Nashville, Geneva, Canterbury, Wheaton, Pirate's Cove, or even Constantinople. Christians in general, that is. It's just that Rome already has the aphorism, and it works better in opposition. Rome versus Carthage. That's what it's all about.

"In other words, we must either believe in God, or else we are compelled to believe in absolutely nothing at all. We can't be even vaguely spiritual, or speak of the universe wanting us to do or to have things. If we, for one moment, open the door to admit even one small angel – or just a window, to admit even the smallest of ghosts – then we are in grave danger of it all unraveling, and suddenly, there we are in Rome, singing along in the village choir."

Illuminata jumped in as Rod stopped. "I disagree. I think there's a lot of things we don't know. We have to approach this with a measure of humility. I'm not so arrogant as to think that I was born into exactly the right culture, at exactly the right time, in exactly the right place. How improbable is that? For me just to be in the right place?"

"If there is a 'right culture,' that is, one that gives rise to a 'right religion,' then it follows that someone, somewhere, has to be born into it, and it's no less likely that it's you, than that it's a remote lama in the Himalayas, or an Incan cleric in the Andes," said Dr. D.

"I resent that idea," she said. "How can you possibly say that? How can you even think it, in this day and age? That's so arrogant, so ethnocentric, I simply have no words for it. I can't imagine the immense egotistical arrogance it would take to say something like that."

"It is what it is," he said, shrugging his shoulders. He leaned forward slightly to see her around Jake, and Jake leaned back slightly to facilitate eye contact. "It's either Rome or Carthage. Anything else is just a waypoint."

"So if I don't want to be a Nihilist, I have to be a Christian? Is that your point? Those are your Rome and Carthage?"

"Precisely. Those are the two logically defensible positions, to which one may be led by logic. And there is only one axiom, one small assumption, separating the two."

"I can't accept that," she said. "There are far more points of view than that. I mean, there is obviously more to this world than just what we see. We can't just arrogantly say that what we see is all we get. But instead, you think the only other choice is that entire old Christian idea of heaven and hell? No, thank you. I'd rather not.

"When I had Ima Gine, the day she was born, that's when it occurred to me that there is nothing she could ever say or do that would lead me to shut her out of my life. I would never say, 'Go away from me and never come back,' and I can never see God just shutting his children away from him forever. It doesn't make sense to me. I've never been to church since."

Jake thought of asking whether everyone is a child of God by birthright; after all, John 1:12 says that one may become a child of God, and strictly speaking, one may only *become* what one is not already. He also thought of pointing out that it is the damned who reject God, and not He them; with hell simply being the only place that is outside of His presence.

But before he had time to choose either theodicy, Rod replied. "I'm not so sure of that," he said. "Your idea that you would never reject your child. What if you had another child, and the first was, as one example, using intravenous drugs. Or doing something else that brought danger into the house. I can see, certainly, a mother kicking out an older child in order to protect a younger child."

Illuminata was furious with this idea, and let Rod know it. How dare he? She protested that he didn't know her at all, and

15

couldn't possibly judge her maternal skills. Besides, the war on drugs was simply a travesty, and there was absolutely no way that her precious child…

Jake got up and walked two steps to the rail, letting the two combatants have direct contact without him in the middle. What had Somers dumped him into?

Behind them, on the fourth and final wooden bench, sat the middle-aged woman in purple, whom Jake had seen on the train. Apparently she, too, was a member of the OAR. Unless, of course, the boat was supposed to dock somewhere else after dropping them off.

He wondered for a moment if he were misreading her. She might possibly be a kindly grandmother. Perhaps she was angry, or perhaps she suffered from some sort of ailment that gave her a displeased look. She met Jake's casual glance with an acidic glare, and he turned his eyes back to the foggy haze.

A small bus had met them at the Emeryville Amtrak station, and had driven them to a nearby dock, where this boat had been waiting. It had a tiny wheelhouse, in which a pilot and one other man sat. It was barely larger than one of those old-fashioned phone booths Jake remembered from when he was very small.

The rest of the boat was a flat wooden deck with an open shelter over hard wooden benches. It was clearly built for utility, and not for comfort.

Jake imagined it being used on sunny days to show sea life to sixth-grade field trips, or to show tourists around Alcatraz, but it seemed like a poor choice to ferry cold travelers across to an island in the dead of wintry night. For one thing, it lacked heat, and the sea breeze sliced through Jake's jacket. It also lacked any sort of light, compelling the passengers to strain their eyes to see each other.

Jake had the impression of sitting on someone's back porch in the dark, awaiting a promised dinner that was indefinitely delayed. It was uncomfortable to both the body and the soul.

The verbal duel soon abated, with Illuminata retiring to sit next to the purple matron, while Rod joined him at the rail.

"You see," he said. "You can take the girl out of Rome, but you can't take Rome out of the girl. She wants the immutable rules of Rome, and also the freedom from rules found only in Carthage." He gestured vaguely towards Illuminata.

"That's what's wrong with atheism today," he continued. "It's all about emotions, and what people feel to be true, and how people feel that this is unjust, or that is unjust. They never follow it through to the logical conclusion. None of that stuff matters to them."

"Justice and feelings don't matter to you at all?"

"Not for those of us who live in Carthage. You remember our sacrifices, don't you?"

Jake did. *Why must we meet in Carthage, with blood upon the ground? Canterbury's neater and a cleaner, greener town. Rome is nice this time of year, and Nashville has its charm; Why must we meet in Carthage where the children come to harm?*

"Nice," said Rod. "Did you just now make that up?"

"Afraid so. Your verse earlier about a party in the old-town Punic square, that must have triggered it."

"Not bad for off-the-cuff, but the meter's a little stilted. Won't scan very well at all, and of course it's the reciprocal of my original theme."

"As you said earlier, we who are from Rome must take the opposite side of that question."

"Touché," said Rod. "I am hoist on my own petard." He stared at Jake in the near darkness. "I think I like you, Jacobs."

The boat nosed up to a dock, scraping along the side. The men in the wheelhouse emerged to throw ropes over the pilings and draw the boat to rest, not bothering with fenders.

A gate was opened, and a small platform was thrown down for a gangplank. It seemed stable enough, and after the ride across the bay, Jake would have slid down a mooring line to escape the hard bench seats. Jake and Rod waited as the Purple matron was helped off by the pilot and his silent partner.

She said a few words to each of them, and it quickly became apparent that this was the very worst boat on the planet, and that they were the very worst crew; this was the very worst dock on the very worst bay; and that had she a chance to do so, she'd have had them all to gaol, the gallows or the guillotine.

Jake offered his arm for Illuminata to steady herself as she stepped off, but she simply gave him haughty look and made her way onto the dock. Jake and Rod followed along.

"I'm not very familiar with the Bay," said Jake, to Rod, the last person from the boat who appeared to still be on speaking terms with him. "Where are we, exactly?"

"Red Rock Island," said Rod, smoothing his greatcoat and gesturing into the fog. "Do you see those lights there?"

"I believe so…"

The lights in question were like a faint string of dim yellow globes, hanging in the fog. There were maybe a dozen in total, dimming with distance until they disappeared altogether. Whiter globes of light, sometimes a bright blue-white, appeared near the farthest yellow globe, and moved across their view, blinking more and more rapidly, and then finally vanishing.

"That is the Richmond-San Rafael bridge over there. And highway 580. We're nearly beneath it. On a clear day, it would be quite obvious. And very near. Almost right on top of us."

"This is the little red island…"

"That one can see from the bridge, yes. We bought it a few years ago — well, that is, there's an agreement in place, you see, with the owners; it's a very complex escrow arrangement. You know how these things are."

Jake had no idea at all of how real estate transactions are, and it made no difference to him. He preferred not to know any of the details. "In driving over that bridge, I'm sure I've never seen a dock on this island," he said.

"There's never been one. It's new. And so is the house at the peak, though we made it with the appearance of age. At some point there's going to be a fight with the powers-that-be over the construction of it, and we want to be able to relate it to the old shack built here in the 1930s.

"We need grounds to say that it's all been grandfathered in. Grounds to say that it was always here on the grounds, if you'll pardon the pun. There's a method in the madness, and there's madness in the method."

"I am intrigued," said Jake, as they joined the others in a small motor-drawn cart, like something that might ferry golfers around from hole to hole on a large golf course. Except that from the general construction of this particular cart, Jake might expect the course to include a windmill hazard.

"Those," he said, "Are things like that make me very glad not to be a lawyer. I've never understood real estate."

The man who had served as the pilot's helper, as they were crossing the bay, now scurried up to the enclosure at the front of the cart and started the engine. It puffed, coughed, and sputtered, settling at last into a slightly loping gait.

"Well, you're not a lawyer in that sense of the word," said Rod. "But you must surely deal with the occasional incident of church law. Is it not so?"

"We Baptists are maybe somewhat lax – or rather, informal, that's probably a better word for it – in our system of polity, I'm afraid. I can't remember the last time a big bylaws issue arose."

"No rulings on whether to wear cotton and wool on the same day? No questions of whether eel is kosher or haram? No debates over how many angels may dance at one time, on the head of a single pin?"

"Not really things we deal with much. That's more on the legalistic side. We try to avoid the ditches and stay in the middle of the road; neither legalistic nor licentious."

The motorized cart, a home-built affair by the looks of it, with a badly underpowered engine and a haphazard power train, labored around narrow switchbacks as it struggled up the steep hill. It was mainly a crude metal box on wheels, with benches in it, very similar in design to the boat that had brought them across the bay.

Where the boat had had a narrow wheelhouse, on the cart there was a transparent plastic partition. Beyond it, in what appeared to be an acrylic box, sat the driver and former mariner. Jake thought he could see a hood extending past the driver, and there did seem to be a pair of headlights, though all they lit up was the dense fog itself.

The engine groaned and strained, leading to jerky transitions at each switchback. The driver ground the gears slightly, adding to the noise. Jake wondered why they hadn't built the house lower, or else brought an actual car from the mainland.

"I don't suppose—" said Jake, but he was cut off by the woman in purple.

"Must you two chatter like magpies?" she snapped. "This is the very worst place for such a conference. And the very worst timing, with this weather. And now, having to listen to the two of you! Imagine!"

Rod turned to Jake. "Forgive her," he said. "If we were serving German sausage, she would surely say that it was the very worst wurst."

Jake was fairly certain that he heard the woman spit. The rest of the ride was silent, cold, and otherwise uneventful. The house atop the hill grew ever nearer; a dark and brooding hulk that sometimes loomed over them in the fog.

At last they reached a level place, and the carriage, if it may be called that, shuddered to a stop beneath a *porte-cochère*. The driver dismounted and let down the near rail, like a sideways tailgate, and then began helping the passengers down.

They were all treated to a bit more purple prose concerning the very worst of things, as the large lady dismounted. Jake, for all of his weariness at the very worst dialog, appreciated that she had, at the very least, not slipped into profanity. He had heard his share of it, and was not offended by it, but he respected those who could keep it out of their normal speech.

Rod led the way up a set of stone steps, where an ornate door presented itself. It was immense, and carved of a dark wood with a curious tiger-sawn grain. It was gothic, exceedingly tall, and seemed as if it might be the main gate to an ancient walled city. He expected some sort of armed guard in classical armor, armed with hoplae or pilae.

"We arrive at the gates of Carthage, where we may hope that Queen Dido waits within, libations for the valiant warriors in her beloved hand," Rod said, working the door latch and using his shoulder to push the door open. "Let all abandon hope who enter herein."

Instead of throngs of Syrio-Phoenician pagans, clamoring for Roman blood, they found a pleasant white marble hallway, lit by sconces along the walls. Statues and huge vases lined the hallway, among doorways extending to the left and the right. It looked a bit like a movie set of a mansion, from a 1930s movie.

Jake stood for a moment, getting his bearings, while Rod and the purple lady began removing their coats. The driver of the ersatz carriage dashed in behind them, closed the front door, and extended his arm in front of himself. As smoothly as he had transformed himself from boatswain to their driver, he transformed again and became a butler.

"May I take your coats?" he asked. One by one, they piled their cloaks and coverings upon him. "Second door to the left, that's where they are. The rest of them, I mean. Of you. Your group, that is."

He vanished, taking the coats with him, presumably to a closet or coat check room of some sort. Jake had a fleeting idea of the man simply stealing them, and he chuckled to himself. As odd as this event was turning out to be so far, it would hardly have surprised him.

The purple-lady, now in a purple dress, pushed past the procrastinating party and proceeded promptly to the designated door. She angrily yanked it open, raised her chin, and marched inside. Rod followed. Jake motioned for Illuminata to precede him, if she wished, but she simply shook her head at him. Shrugging, he walked in.

A fire burned in the immense fireplace, hissing and roaring as it drew air up through the stacked wood on the grate, and sent its flames dancing up into the flue. It seemed inviting, even charming, after the chill and dark outside.

Two old men sat near it, in blue wingback chairs that were covered in an odd patterned cloth. It appeared to feature tiny yellow birds, or perhaps winged fish, against a background that varied in hue from royal blue to a deep indigo. The general effect was that the chairs had been made to be overly expensive and slightly unsightly.

One of the men seemed impossibly old. He was tall and narrow, his parchment skin nearly transparent, and the bones of his hand were clearly visible as ridges underneath. For that matter, his veins left little to the imagination, showing faintly as blue serpentines woven through the bones, and one of his arteries pulsed weakly but visibly in the thin webbing between his thumb and first finger.

He was bald, and his long face was entirely shaved, as if no hair had ever grown there, despite his age. His face turned down into a permanent frown, as if he disapproved of everything and of everyone.

The second man seemed impossibly round, as if he were made to be the exact opposite of the first man. Jake's immediate thought, one for which he rebuked himself, were of a cue stick and a cue ball. The rounder man had hair, dyed black, as if to hide his age. His face gave the trick away at once: He had the long rolling wrinkles of a man who has seen many seasons.

His arms were folded across his middle, where no clear line separated thorax from abdomen. Jake had a quick thought of Nero Wolfe, but this man was not dressed in yellow and brown, nor did anything in his face suggest intelligence.

The two old men, who seemed to have been deep in some sort of discussion, simply acknowledged the new arrivals with a dismissive wave of their hands, before going back to their drinks and conversation.

"May I quickly get everyone drinks?" said the servant, who was also the driver, and had just taken their coats. He gave the air of being in a hurry to carry out his checklist of tasks.

"Scotch and soda," said the purple lady. "Light on the soda. And where's the supper?"

"Simmering," he said, with a glance towards the adjacent doorway, where a dining table had been set. "The cook and I must make our boat back, and the second set of servers will be returning shortly. Shift change."

"Unacceptable," hissed the purple lady.

"Gin and tonic, if I may," said Rod.

"Red wine if you have it," said Illuminata. "White if you don't. Or a grey Zin."

The servant nodded and dashed towards the kitchen.

"Introductions are in order," said the round man, paying attention to the new arrivals at last, and assuming the air of a master of ceremonies. "I am Arley Ashton, of Seattle South College of Technology." He motioned to the thin man.

"Carlisle Guthrie," he gasped. "And before you ask, no, not one of *those* Guthries." He sipped his drink, signifying that he was done speaking.

"I am Doctor Marcion, of the University of California at Salinas," said the lady in purple. Every word was like a small explosion, as if it were an imposition to make her say them. "UCS, they had to give it those initials, so everyone thinks I'm down at USC, the University of Spoiled Children."

Jake recognized her name, and almost remarked that she might know one of his parishioners, Dr. Winter. He caught his tongue at the last moment. Dr. Winter might not like his name being dragged into her drama.

"Now, Doctor," said Rod, "I'm sure that the Regents of the University of California did not intend it as a personal slight. By the way, is there a first name by which we may call you?"

"I have one, but you just try calling me by it," she snapped. "And just who are you, anyway?"

"Rodel Dobrazamery, of the University of Prague, on loan to the California Institute of Technology. Call me Rod. I am a medical doctor, but for the present time, I teach Italian poets."

"I doubt they learn much," snapped Marcion.

Jake cleared his throat. "I'm Jake Jacobs, and please call me Jake. I'm to be the keynote speaker, which I'm told is something of a sacrificial lamb."

"SJ?" gasped Guthrie.

"SBC," said Jake. "I'm standing in for Father Somers."

"Just like a Jesuit to slip off into the night," said Ashton.

"Father Somers is Episcopalian, not Jesuit, I'm afraid."

"Just like a Jesuit not to be one," said Guthrie.

"Oh, dear, you're all starting already, and we haven't even had our drinks," said Illuminata. "If you must, call me Nata. I'm Dr. Illuminata McMurray, of the Los Angeles City University, Northern Arrondissement."

"We have arrondissements in Los Angeles?" asked Marcion, with venom in her eyes and on her tongue.

"Only in the minds of our board of directors." She accepted a glass of red wine from the all-purpose servant. "One of them may have visited Paris once, I have to assume."

The servant gave a GT to Rod, offered a scotch and soda to Marcion, and then turned a speculative eye to Jake.

"Nothing for me," said Jake. "If I feel dry before the others return, I'll grab a glass of water from the kitchen."

"Bless you," breathed the servant, before vanishing into the dining room in a blur.

"There's way too much soda in this," snapped Marcion, "And not nearly enough scotch." Her warranty call was in vain, however, as the butler and driver was gone.

There was a crash of thunder, surprisingly audible in the small mansion. The crystal chandelier in the dining room rattled furiously, then began to softly sway.

"I hope that wasn't something blowing up," said Illuminata.

"I hope it was that awful boat, with all of them onboard," muttered Marcion. "They are the very worst."

Chapter Three

They'll party through the evening,
With their hands up in the air;
And in the morning wake again,
In dread and dark despair.

"THEY'VE BEEN GONE A long time," said Guthrie.

"Quite poor form to leave us alone with not even a single servant," said Ashton. He took an *hors d'ouevre* from the tray on the low table. "How are we to get fresh drinks?"

"I suppose that they had a shift-change of some sort," said Jake. "Labor laws, that sort of thing."

"We'll fire the company that provides them," said Guthrie. "Labor laws. Who ever heard of such a thing?" He stared at the tray of *hors d'ouevres* as if he expected one to crawl across the room and bite him.

"Dinner needs to be soon, or the directors will hear of it," said Marcion. "This is quite a slap in the face."

"Maybe they had trouble with the boat," said Illuminata. She helped herself to a *crudité* from the second, slightly smaller tray. It appeared to be a white spread of some sort in a sliver of mild pepper. "These are quite tasty."

"They're not really. They just seem like it because we're all starving," said Marcion.

"It was most kind of Jake, then, to go in and bring these from the kitchen," said Illuminata.

Marcion was trapped. She either had to thank Jake for his kindness, or else stop complaining. Anything else would reveal her as petty and self-contradictory. She glared at Illuminata, for putting her into this spot. It was like a slap in the face.

"Now I'm starting to wonder if we should maybe serve ourselves dinner," suggested Jake. "I imagine that the boat may have had a small problem. It could be a while."

"Maybe they had a flat rudder," mused Rod. "Or ran out of whatever it is that runs those things."

"I was thinking more along the lines of getting lost in the fog, or having to reduce their speed," said Jake.

"Right," said Rod. "That would explain it, too."

"We could at least manage the soup course by ourselves," said Illuminata. "It shouldn't be too hard to do that. I doubt the servants would mind, when they finally get here."

"We could say that the last crew said to do it," said Guthrie.

"Are any of us qualified to serve soup?" asked Ashton.

"I worked in a diner during college," said Jake. "To pay for my last two years. I just might be able to manage it."

"Oh, one of the working class," said Guthrie. "I can't wait for your keynote speech. It should be utterly charming."

"Should we vote on serving ourselves?" asked Illuminata.

"No, Marcion will just complain," said Rod. "Let's do it."

"While you're in there dishing the soup," said Ashton, "Let's find out if anyone's qualified to do something with this fire. It's not working very well." He scowled at the logs, now reduced to ends and embers.

"I believe one is meant to throw on another log," said Rod. "It's what we do in Prague."

Jake missed the remainder of the dialog about the fire, as he slipped into the kitchen in search of bowls.

Guthrie gave a chuckle. He held up a small tablet. "There's some fool on the NewMedia app who doesn't know that Jesus was a obviously just a myth. Oh, you'll all just have to pardon me for a moment, but I must set her straight immediately."

Ashton laughed. "He loves it when someone is wrong on the internet. It makes his day."

"Calls herself NoVowelPSW. I'm sure we're meant to know what that means," chuckled Guthrie. "It's some vague Christian thing, maybe. Maybe it's a sin to say, 'I,' or some such folly."

"I think I debated her a week ago," said Nata. "She seemed to know a bit about history and literature, but kept insisting that morality needs a base. Even quoted from Euthyphyro. I did, I confess, find that promising."

"Euthyphyro. Hmph. We make our own history, our own literature, our own morals, and our own truth," pronounced Marcion. "We have no need of gods for that. What do they add, can anyone tell me? What problem do they solve?"

"I wonder if PSW stands for some kind of social warrior." mused Rod. "Might be an enlightened Christian."

"If so, the P must be for pigheaded," said Ashton. "Or it's for prudish, pretentious, preposterous, or puerile. Pointless?"

"Speaking of things that are pointless, I find this insistence upon electronic amusements to be a bit out of place," sniffed Marcion. "We should be able to talk amongst ourselves without digital helpers."

"Point taken," said Guthrie. "I'll turn this thing off once I smite this theist. It needs to be done."

"You can't wait until you retire for the evening?" asked Marcion. "It's like a slap in the face."

"At my age, one does things while one may," said Guthrie.

"Where's that fellow with the soup?" asked Ashton.

"Probably putting poison in it," muttered Marcion.

"I'll just pop in to see what's keeping him." Rod rose and made his way through the ornate dining room into the kitchen. In keeping with the Victorian theme, the kitchen had been made just like that of an old manor house: It centered around a huge ancient wood-burning stove.

Rod arrived to find Jake shoving sticks of wood into a hole in the front of the stove. Two deep pots of murky liquids bubbled on the black iron stovetop.

"Those would be the long-awaited soups, I suppose," said Rod. "What can I do to help?"

"Well, I found a matching pair of tureens," said Jake. "I suppose that the soup is intended to be served from them. Now we just need ladles and bowls."

"I suppose we should see who wants which before we dish it out," said Rod. "What are our choices?"

Jake pointed to the pot on the right. "That seems to be French onion," he said, "And the other is kind of an artichoke puree. But with something else in it, also. I don't have the palate to tell what it is, exactly. Leeks, maybe."

"Do you think we should call them into the dining room, to sit at dinner formally, or simply serve them where they lie?"

"The simplest would be to put both tureens in the dining room, and let them serve themselves," said Jake. "But I imagine there's little chance of that."

"Anything interesting in the oven?"

"Looks like a kind of a chicken cobbler. Eight all together, in small proofing pans. They've got a ways to go, from the looks of them. I think the fire may have burned down a bit more than was intended." He stoked the fire a bit more, uncertain how to gauge the level of heat.

"A small serving of fowl apiece. Yes, that'll be for the first main course, no doubt. I'll go and get orders for the soups, and we can carry out the bowls on a tray," said Rod. "You might find bowls and spoons in the cabinet up there."

He was back in a moment, with a small notepad. "Four french onion, and one artichoke — make it two; I'll have the artichoke as well. And whatever you're having, of course."

"That adds up to seven orders, counting us. I only saw six of us earlier. Did I miss someone?"

28

"Oh, yes. Ulysses awakened."

"That sounds like the title of an epic poem. I guess I may have missed his arrival."

"He's always around. I think he's a Vietnam vet. Likes to snooze in a chair in the drawing room. I'm not sure if he's really a member, or if he was on the construction crew and just stayed on with us. He came with the house, so to speak."

"Maybe he got lost on the way home, like his namesake. If it took him ten years to get home from 'Nam, though, he'd have gotten there by '85 or so, at least."

"Ha. Good point. No nymphs holding him captive here, and I doubt that Penelope would still be waiting up for him."

The soups were served, in fine china bowls, on matching saucers, carried to the parlor on brown oval bakelite trays. The various attendees reacted in different ways.

Ashton and Guthrie each ignored the offering, allowing it to be set on stands or tables by them. Ulysses took the saucer in his hand, and attacked the soup with a fury. Marcion gave a haughty *Harumph!* to herald the sauce. Illuminata offered a soft *Hvala* to Rod, as he handed her a bowl of the artichoke.

As Jake lowered himself into a chair and picked up his bowl, Marcion cleared her throat.

"Is there no pepper?" she asked.

"Excuse," said Rod. "I have it here." He quickly drew a small pepper grinder from his jacket pocket and proffered it to Marcion, who stared at it in dismay.

"Am I supposed to grind it myself?"

"Perish the thought," said Rod, with an indulgent smile. He stood and ground pepper above her bowl.

"Stop, that's way too much. You've ruined it," she said. "It's like a slap in the face. One thing after another. What else can possibly go wrong?"

Jake thought of two or three responses, discarded each, and took to his soup in earnest. The onion soup was very savory, and the onions were well caramelized. The seasoning was on point, and the slices of cheese toast he had found in the smaller oven were perfectly sized for the bowls.

He had sampled the artichoke earlier, partly to find out what it was, and while it seemed heavenly, he had gone with the alternative. He was not disappointed: the onion soup was so good that he emptied his bowl almost instantly.

He looked up, and saw the others barely beginning, or else sipping daintily. Only Ulysses had finished. Jake nodded to him.

"I'm going back for a second round," he said. "Can I refill yours while I'm up?"

"Yeah," said Ulysses, in a gruff voice. "But Artichoke this time. To see if it's any better."

Jake refilled the bowls, pausing to check on the chicken cobblers. The oven gave a slight chicken scent, and lattices were showing the very slightest trace of color at the edges. He supposed that he had time to eat his soup before they would be ready. Bowls in hand, he went back to the parlor.

"Well," said Guthrie, sipping his soup. "That explains why the servants aren't back yet."

"What does?"

"I just received an email from the agency. Apparently we failed to pay their bill. The servants are all suspended as of midnight. Which was just about the time that the outgoing boat would have docked at Richmond."

"They should be doing this for the good of mankind," snapped Marcion. "We are advancing rationality and reason in the face of religion and home-schooling. We are bringing about the advent of the *ubermensch*, for the good of humanity."

"Well, all is not lost," said Ashton. "If the boat can be summoned back to pick up us all up, we can be at *La Belle Dame Sans Delicatesse*, that new bistro in the city, in time for a late supper and midnight snack." He licked his lips at the thought.

"That's a problem," said Guthrie. "The servants were our point-of-contact. No one else knows the number for the boat."

"Can't we get another service?"

"I suppose we might, but we can't call. My cell phone's just stopped working." He held it to his ear and shook it, as if that might start it running. He poked at it with his finger, swiped this way and that, and then put it to his ear again.

"Mine too," said Ashton.

"Silly question, but did we pay that bill?" asked Rod.

"Apparently not." Marcion hurled her cell phone into the fireplace, where it shattered; its fragmented remains falling among the embers. The lithium battery deflagrated furiously, ascending the chimney as a puff of white smoke.

"That's not safe to do," said Guthrie, glaring at her. "That's made from lithium. It's not supposed to be disposed of in fire. Don't you read instruction manuals?"

"Don't tell me what to do!" she shouted, seizing the cell phone on the nearest end table and hurling it after the first phone, with similar results.

"That was mine," said Jake. "And I still had a signal."

"Just put it into your expenses," advised Rod. He shrugged and hurled his own phone into the fireplace. "As they say, when in Rome…"

"Do as the Carthaginians?"

"Something like that."

Chapter Four

THE ONLINE APOLOGIST WHOM they referred to as NoVowelPSW, known to her friends as Bryly Jacobs, noticed that the anti-theists she had been debating all suddenly dropped offline, all at once. She knew that she shouldn't smite the infidels in online debates, but it seemed impossible to avoid.

Everywhere she looked, someone was saying something so absolutely silly that she couldn't resist trying to set the record straight. Tonight, it seemed to be the "Christmas is pagan" theme. She knew better than to engage them. She really did.

The lull – curiously just at midnight – brought her to her senses. It was time to go to sleep. Procrastination wasn't helping anything. Normally, she and Jake would have gone to bed an hour ago, or even two, but his absence, and the brewing storm, had left her slightly agitated.

Bryly slowly climbed the stairs, looking forward to the day when she would suddenly be lighter and more flexible. At the top of the stairs, instead of walking to the room she shared with Jake, she instead opened the door of the proposed nursery. The crib was there, against an inside wall, and a large rocker stood opposite it. The walls had been freshly painted – part of Bryly's nesting phase – and colorful decal images of cartoon characters decorated the ceiling.

She mentally went through the checklist of items to prepare before Faith arrived, though she had counted them off dozens, or possibly hundreds, of times already. The paints were all non-toxic, check; the crib was safety rated, with slats less than four inches apart, check; and there was even a fire extinguisher.

It was just a matter of waiting, and it was down to days; maybe even hours. Bryly was tired of waiting. She was tired of being tired of waiting.

Faith, the expected child, wasn't making it any easier. As if she sensed her mother's anxiety, the baby had been moving constantly. Turning handsprings, or so it seemed to Bryly. She wondered for the ten-thousandth time if she and Jake were up to the task of raising a child.

She knew better, but in her mind she imagined Faith emerging as an over-active and precocious toddler, crayons in hand, racing to and fro, finding new and clever ways to start trouble and break things.

Some anxiety is normal, she told herself, as she made her way to her own bed. *And nothing that we worry about is likely to go as badly as we fear.* She said things like this to her clients in the office all the time, but it struck her as much different to be saying it to herself. She sighed at the irony and put it out of her mind.

Bryly climbed into bed, turned off the light, and began a lengthy prayer for the baby, and for the safety of her husband, that he would be protected at all times from every manner of evil. And somewhere around there, she fell asleep.

Jake, for his part, was serving the chicken cobblers. The lattice tops had become a golden brown, no doubt the result of a painstaking egg-wash applied by the first-shift servants. The proofing pans were each about a third the size of the chicken pies Jake was accustomed to, but these had apparently been intended to only serve as a first main course, and not as the dinner entrée itself.

Unfortunately, neither Jake nor Rod had been able to find any other prepared food. As a result, the late meal came to a screeching halt after the pies. Jake supposed that the relief cook and all-purpose stewards would have had the remaining courses with them when they arrived on the boat, but he had no idea how these sorts of dinners were normally prepared. His culinary knowledge was very basic, and was centered more on serving and eating than on the necessary cooking.

Rod had graciously offered to dish up the rest of the soup, for those still hungry, but except for Jake and Ulysses, the offer had fallen onto deaf ears.

Having eaten all the available comestibles, and having lost the internet connection, they found themselves staring into the fire, or looking at each other in uncomfortable silence. Rod finally stood and addressed them.

"Since Jake so very kindly took on the roles of cook and servant this evening, it hardly seems sporting to subject him to our normal game of ridiculing and abusing the speaker. If I may, I would instead like to collect your opinions on a topic near and dear to our own hearts."

"I'd like a cherry cheesecake near to my heart, about where my stomach is," said Ashton.

"Be that as it may, please indulge me. Suppose that you were about to be killed unless you can offer a morally sufficient reason that he should not. What words would you say, to save your life?"

"Well," said Marcion, rolling her eyes, "If you have to ask, you're too silly to be a member here. We pride ourselves on being smart enough not to ask silly questions."

"Do humor me, please," said Rod. "Blame it, if you will, on an error in the translation from my mother tongue."

"Morally sufficient reason? Ha. You're a human. Murder is just evil. It's wrong. Every fully functioning human knows that. If I have to explain to you why it's wrong, then you're not a fully functioning human yourself." She crossed her arms and stared daggers at him.

"It is counterproductive to the thriving of humanity," said Ashton. "We can't expect to build a human society that can reach the stars if we're killing each other."

"Social contract," said Guthrie. "I've given up my right to kill you in exchange for the right not to be killed by you. We wish to live safely, and that can only be accomplished by making it safe to live among us." He turned in his chair, facing Ulysses. "Of course, I'm dying to hear from Odysseus on this."

"My namesake would have told you that the one must surrender his rights for the many, and would have told how the son of Peleus wreaked havoc by not putting the common good above his own pride." He yawned. "But for me, it's more about Kant. I'm not going to make a rule for everyone to commit murder, so I'm not going to murder."

"Admirable," said Guthrie. "But what if someone wishes to murder you, and doesn't mind it being a general rule?"

"I'd say he hasn't read his Kant."

"A nice spectrum of ideas thus far," said Rod. "And how about you, Illuminata? What would you say?"

"You're trying to draw me into another argument, like you did on the boat. I won't have it."

"Oh, be a dear and play along," said Ashton.

"It's only fair; we all gave our thoughts," said Guthrie.

"Alright, then, if I really must. Empathy. All morality is simply empathy. I would appeal to the killer's empathy. If we have any emotion at all, any feeling for others, any decency, any understanding that others are just like us… Well, then we know we must not kill each other."

"Thank you," said Rod. "And Jake, I suppose that you follow the moral dictum, *Thou shall not kill?*"

"Well, with some nuances."

"There are always nuances," chuckled Ashton. "Prepare to see a dazzling display of mental gymnastics."

"First, the verse in Exodus, 3:20 I believe, is much better translated as *Thou shall not murder.*"

"Tomato, potato," said Marcion.

"Second, the principle is better stated in Genesis 9:6. *Whoever shall kill a man, by mankind shall he be killed, for he is made in the image of God.*"

"Is there no mention anywhere in that holy book of yours of someone killing – or, excuse me, of murdering – a woman?" asked Illuminata. "When you get around to asking me why I'm not a Christian, Jake, that sort of deeply-embedded misogyny is going to be part of the answer."

"Man, as used here, is mankind, as opposed to animals. The ancient Hebrew language did not distinguish mankind from an individual man. Thus, the somewhat misogynistic sound of that verse, in our own modern ears. But, of course, that's merely an artifact of translation. All humans on earth are covered by the Noahite prohibition on murder."

"So then it's perfectly okay to kill all of the animals, is it?" snapped Marcion. "Just wipe them out?"

"You didn't object to the chicken cobbler earlier," said Rod. "So that can't be too big an issue for you."

"To clarify my answer," said Jake, "My reason for it to be wrong to kill me would be that I am a bearer of the image of God. The word-picture here relates to the image of a king, worn around the neck of an ambassador, to show just who it was whom he represented."

"Oh," said Guthrie, "Lovely. You're God's ambassador, so we mere mortals can't touch you. Isn't that nice?"

"Not what I said," replied Jake. "We all bear the *Imago Dei*."

"I, for one, refuse to wear anything with an image of your stone-age goat-herder's God," said Marcion.

"It merely means that we each have attributes that resemble God's attributes," said Jake.

"We said that we weren't going to besiege poor Jake," said Illuminata. "Not after he was so kind as to serve us dinner."

"If you call that a dinner," muttered Marcion.

"So, Doctor Dobrazamery," asked Illuminata, shifting in her chair to better face him, "What is your answer – The true and correct answer, no doubt?"

"I'm glad you asked," he said, in a didactic tone. "If one follows the atheist worldview to its logical conclusion–"

"It's not a worldview!" snapped Guthrie. "It's merely the absence of a belief."

Rod rolled his eyes. "If one follows the train to the end of the line, to the terminal station, Kafka and Nietzsche are there to carry one's bags."

"Don't be silly," said Ashton. "You're going to say that he shouldn't kill you because you're some kind of *ubermensch?*"

"Not at all," said Rod. "I'd tell the killer that he has no reason not to kill me. No reason at all."

Chapter Five

IT WAS AROUND THREE in the morning when Jake remembered the eighth chicken cobbler. Seven were served, and the last one was left in the oven. And that was a problem.

One might be forgiven for thinking that perhaps Jake went downstairs in the hope of eating it. The thought had, in fact, crossed his mind, but his sense of fairness dismissed it.

But it had also crossed his mind that the oven, left unattended for all these hours, might have made charcoal of the pie, and might be spewing clouds of smoke into the kitchen. Or might even have set the kitchen on fire, unlikely as it seemed.

He threw a bathrobe over his pajamas, put on his shoes like slippers, and trotted down the stairs. In the marble hallway, his footsteps echoed a slapping sound with every step. The sconces had been turned out, but a single lamp by the parlor door cast a small yellow pool of light.

He hurried to the service door and pushed through, into the kitchen. It was dark, and Jake was pleased not to smell smoke. He flicked on the light switch, and immediately noticed two things: First, that the last small chicken pie was gone from the wide-open oven.

And also, that Ulysses was lying sprawled on the kitchen floor in a pool of blood.

It took only the slightest touch to confirm that Ulysses was dead. No living person could be so cold as the skin of Ulysses. Except possibly Marcion. Jake immediately rebuked himself for that slightly uncharitable, if arguably true, thought.

His normal reaction on discovering a body would be to call the police. There was little hope of that, with his cell phone quietly melting in the embers of the parlor fireplace.

He remembered someone saying that the island was clearly visible, even obvious, from the San Rafael bridge. He thought of going out and trying to signal passing cars, if there were any. A glance at the window dispelled any hope. A fog, thicker and murkier than the artichoke soup – and perhaps with a stronger flavor – lurked outside, obscuring all.

If he found a powerful flashlight, and managed to signal the bridge, at best the passersby might see a vague flashing glow. Also, Jake only remembered a few letters of Morse code. He doubted that anyone else on the island knew more. And even then, they'd be reliant upon a driver who understood the distress signal. Things were beginning to look bleak.

A clock in the parlor struck the hour. By that clock, it should be three-fifteen AM, assuming that it worked better than most things on this island. He wondered if he should wake the others, if only to make sure that Ulysses was the only one among them to have a dramatic shift in body temperature.

He also wondered if he should go back to bed. He doubted he'd get much sleep, but the kitchen was too cold for standing around. But, sadly, he couldn't just pretend he hadn't found a dead body. He had to do something.

He stood for a moment, waiting for an idea to pop into his head, but nothing seemed forthcoming. There was no getting around it. He had to wake the others.

Whatever he was going to do, the first order of business was to change from his pajamas into something warmer. He left the light on, so that no one getting up for a glass of water would trip over Ulysses, and made his way back upstairs.

He heard a loud thump in the parlor, and started to go back down to investigate, but decided against it. If it were nothing, he'd feel silly, and if it were the killer, he'd feel even worse. Or possibly he'd feel nothing at all, ever again.

He took the stairs two at a time, and thought again about his urgent need to lose some weight. He wasn't fat, but he was certainly well-rounded.

He pounded on the next door to his, down the hall.

"Quiet that racket," screeched Marcion.

"Mayhem is afoot," he shouted. "Please get up and meet us all in the parlor!"

The door across the stair opened. Rod's head poked out. "Did I hear a cry of mayhem?" he asked.

"You did indeed," said Jake. "Mord und Totshlag. Chaos is afoot. Would you please dress and meet us all in the parlor?"

Rod's door closed, and Jake glided up the stairs to the next floor. He pounded on the first door he saw. Illuminata yanked it open, as if she had been waiting on the other side.

Jake paused and did a double-take. She was wearing a bright yellow raincoat. It was the same style that children used to wear back in the seventies; some sort of rubberized cloth, with big black toggles up the front to hold it closed. Beads of moisture covered the raincoat, wetting it just to the point where it seemed about to drip onto the floor.

"We're gathering in the parlor," said Jake, while knitting his brow. "There's been a tragic event."

"Like being stuck on an island in a storm?" asked Nata. "Alright, I'll be down directly."

He knocked on the next door as Nata slammed hers. "Can't a man sleep?" shouted Guthrie. "Whatever it is, just deal with it and leave me alone."

"I can't do that," said Jake. "I need everyone in the parlor, for your own safety."

40

"Safety? From what? Next you'll say the roof's caving in. Oh, alright, just go away. I'm coming."

He knocked on the last door, but there was no response. He pounded on it with his fists. "Ashton," he shouted. "Arley Ashton!" After a moment, he beat on the door some more, and then tried the knob.

It was open. He flicked on the light, revealing a bed that had been slept in, but was now vacant. He turned around to find Ashton, fully dressed, standing in the hallway.

"What's all the fuss?" he asked. "Can't a man go visit the 'loo without a hullabaloo?"

"Do you always go to the bathroom fully dressed?"

"Yes, a habit I got into at VMI. And unfortunately, our rooms here don't have sinks."

"Well," said Jake, "Be that as it may, please meet us all in the parlor. There's been a tragedy."

"Always some sort of drama," said Ashton. "And of course it couldn't be a comedy."

Doors were opening on both floors, and Jake followed Nata, who followed Guthrie down the stairs. Ashton came along behind them. At the second floor, Jake ducked into his room, just as Marcion came out of hers and joined the parade.

"Hypocrite!" she screamed. "You're going back to sleep, aren't you? After waking us all!"

When he was changed from his pajamas, Jake dashed down the stairs, almost running into Illuminata.

"Just coming up to see what's holding you," she said, reversing her course. "We'd all like to know why we had to get out of bed so urgently in the middle of the night."

"It'll be better if I explain to all of you once," said Jake, "Rather than one at a time. But, trust me, you'll all be glad that I took the time to wake you."

"I doubt that," she said, as she followed him across the marble hallway and into the parlor.

Heads turned as he entered. Guthrie and Ashton stood near the cold fireplace, as if willing it to light. Nata walked over and poured herself a drink from the wet bar, possibly a ginger ale. Marcion was holding a rocks glass, with about four fingers of what appeared to be unadulterated whiskey.

Rod was kneeling at the hearth, crumpling newspaper from a stack near the fireplace, and turned to Jake as he entered. "*Ecco homo,*" he said, with a smile.

"I'll cut straight to the chase," said Jake. "Ulysses has been murdered, and his body is in the kitchen."

"That's preposterous," said Marcion.

"I doubt that very much," said Guthrie. "He was fine a few hours ago. Wait, was it food poisoning?"

"Tell us what you know," implored Nata.

"I woke up thinking about the last chicken pastry. There was an eighth, and we left it in the oven."

"Not sharing your midnight snack?" asked Ashton. "For shame, Padre. For shame."

"I was more concerned that leaving it in the oven might have turned it into charcoal, or even set it on fire. I didn't want to kill us all in our sleep, with a fire, or with carbon monoxide."

"I assume it didn't catch fire."

"No. As I found it, the oven was open, the pie was gone, and Ulysses was face down on the floor in a pool of his own blood, cold as a penguin and hard as a carp."

"Penguins are actually quite warm beneath their feathers," said Nata. "Between the feathers and a nice layer of fat, they're well insulated. It's one of the reasons that they are hunted by sea lions. The insulating layer, that is. Not the warmth."

"That's good to know," he said. "Anyway, Ulysses has been murdered. He's in the kitchen now. I had to wake you, to make sure the rest of you were okay."

"Afraid of being alone with a killer," sneered Guthrie. "Where's that Christian courage, strolling through the valley of death, all of that nonsense?"

"I was more concerned with stopping the killer from completing any plans he might have had to kill any more of us."

"So, Ulysses is in the kitchen right now?" asked Rod.

"Yes. He won't have moved by himself. I left the light on so nobody would trip over him in the dark."

"In case the rest of us wanted midnight snacks and remembered the eighth pie?" asked Ashton. "You really don't think much of us."

"I didn't actually have a specific case in mind. It was merely a general precaution."

Rod moved to the doorway between the dining room and kitchen. "There's no light on now," he said, pointing to the gap under the door.

"Then someone's been in the kitchen since I went to wake all of you. Or else the bulbs have all burned out."

"Or you had a bad dream," said Marcion. "Brought on by hogging all the food."

"This is easily settled," said Rod. He pushed open the kitchen door and flicked on the lights. The others crowded around him to see.

There was no sign of Ulysses, and the floor was spotless.

Chapter Six

In Rome they sing His praises,
The One whose Name they share;
They speak of peace and righteousness
And of how the holy fare.

They look for One who'll come back soon,
His Name they all declare;
At night they weep for Carthage,
And the ones who perish there.

BRYLY ROLLED OUT OF bed at first light. She had been dreaming of Jake. He was standing on a rock, just wide enough for his feet. Waves sloshed around it, but not quite enough to wet his shoes. He had been singing a hymn, and throwing bits of chicken to a half-dozen hungry crocodiles, who swam in circles around the rock.

No, on second count, there were only five crocks. Jake didn't seem worried – One of his most annoying features was his calmness at times. He just kept singing, and tossing bits of chicken into their greedy mouths.

The hymn was stuck in her head now, even after she was awake. *All other ground is sinking sand, all other ground is sinking sand.* It was from the 1834 hymn by Mote and Bradbury, and she could not, try as she might, remember the rest of the song. Maybe once she'd had coffee, it might come back to her.

It was early, the bed was soft, and the house was cold, but sleeping in wasn't an option. Faith was having none of that: Mommy was getting up, whether she liked it or not.

Bryly found herself looking forward to getting the process over with. It had been exciting at first, and a new adventure. Then it had slowly turned into hard work, lugging the firstborn and her water jacket. But all the sources she had read online said that an active baby was a healthy baby, so she supposed she should be happy.

Maybe after coffee she could convince herself. Throwing a shawl around her shoulders, she made her way downstairs and started the coffee. Faith seemed to have calmed down, so Bryly had a seat in the big living room chair while she waited for it to brew. She pulled a throw blanket from the couch, and spread it over herself. She glanced at the book on the stand beside the chair. It was a gothic murder mystery set in Bavaria. The title was *The Augsburg Confession.*

She had read a similar book by the same author, set in the capital of the Czech Republic. In it, a vital clue had been thrown out a window. That one was called *The Defenestration of Prague.*

Bryly stared at the book for a moment, but she felt too tired to read. With Faith at last calm, she felt as if she were sinking into the chair. *All other ground is sinking sand.* She allowed her eyelids to droop ever so slightly.

In moments, she was snoring.

Jake wished he could snore, or at least doze, but sleep was out of the question at that moment. He was standing in the kitchen, pointing to the blank kitchen floor. "He was there," he said. "His skin was as cold as a polar bear's heart."

"Facing which way?" asked Rod.

"Why does it matter?" snapped Marcion. "Jake probably just saw a body in his dream and thought it was a real person, like all of his hallucinating apostles."

"Except that he would have dreamed that a dead man was alive, not that a live man was dead," said Rod. "There is an easy way to know if Jake's crazy, and it is to find Ulysses. If we find him alive and well, then Jake had a bad dream."

"For the record," said Nata, "The oven is open and the eighth pie is gone. So that checks out, at least."

"So your old flame sleepwalks," said Ashton. "And sleep-eats, also. Hence the missing pie."

"I certainly don't see a body anywhere. Should we declare a miracle and start a religion around it?" snapped Guthrie.

"Let's see if we can find the Ulysses first, before we jump to conclusions, shall we?" asked Rod. "We might be rushing into things, here. He might be asleep somewhere."

"In all the movies they pair up," sniffed Ashton. "To keep an eye on each other. Or protect each other."

"Okay, if it makes you feel better," said Rod. "You and Guthrie, you can be a pair. Nata and Marcion can be a pair. I'll pair up with Jake."

"Why that pairing?" asked Marcion. "Must I be paired with her, of all these people? It's just like a slap in the face. She's the very worst…"

"She's the other female. We wouldn't want the killer to take advantage when you're indisposed."

"There's that, I suppose," said Nata, who was obviously no more pleased than Marcion by the pairing. "But doesn't that mean that one of us must be paired with the killer?"

"Only if Jake was truly right about Ulysses being dead," said Rod. "Then we have a killer among us."

"And by contrast, the killer is paired with one of us," said Jake. "Which might be a just and fitting punishment for murder, all in itself."

"Just like a Jesuit to resort to ad hom," said Ashton.

"That's not an ad hom," said Nata.

"Just like a Jesuit not to be able to make an ad hom," said Guthrie. "But he's not even a Jesuit."

"I know one, if it helps," said Jake. "Maybe I can refer him for next year."

"If we're not all dead by then," said Ashton.

"We should be so lucky," said Marcion.

"On a practical point, why don't Nata and Marcion check the ground floor for Ulysses? Sing out if you find him. Be sure to check all the chairs in the drawing room; he likes to sleep there. And in the parlor, of course."

"Sounds like something you'd say about a pet cat," said Marcion. "I suppose he likes to sleep on the window sill, also."

"Not that we've observed," said Guthrie. "And he never wakes us at night to help him chase imaginary mice."

"No," said Ashton, "But Jake here seems to have awakened us to chase an imaginary body. Or a ghost."

"And its killer," said Nata. "I never realized you had such a feline disposition, Jake. Shall I fetch you a saucer of milk?"

"Enough catty remarks," said Rod. "Ashton, Guthrie, check the sleeping rooms. Start with your own."

The other four atheists divided into pairs and set out on their missions. Rod turned to Jake. "So, I suppose we should take the kitchen apart, then."

"So, Rod," asked Jake, "If we were to catch this killer, what do you suppose we ought to do with him?"

"Good question. One of the best questions of all time, I suppose. I mean, justice must prevail, right? To deter crime, we must punish it, or seem to. We need the noble lie, after all."

"The noble lie? You mean justice?"

"Well, yes. I mean, from an evolutionary standpoint alone, we should be out killing each other. All those of the same sex, that is. Maximizing reproductive ratios."

"And I suppose that women ought to be doing the same?"

"Killing other women, yes, to improve competitive odds."

"Rather counter-productive over all." He started opening large cabinets, of a size suitable for a body. None held bodies.

"Well, exactly, and that's where the noble lie comes in. For a pack, the noble lie is that we're stronger together than we are apart, so we need the rest of the pack. That we'll get along better if we follow the moral code." He peered into a closet and then closed the door again. "Not many places here for Ulysses to be hidden."

"And how does that noble lie work with real humans? People who, though flawed, choose not to spend all their time killing competitors and reproducing?" asked Jake. He scanned the windows, all of which had been painted shut. The paint was unbroken in the corners of the sills.

"With humans, we just call it justice. We say that we're protecting each other for the common good, and we set up all these laws, and courts, and so forth. Thus saith the law, 'Thou shalt not murder, nor manslaughter.' So based on the pretense that we can really achieve justice – that we can lay aside our self interest in order to fairly judge each other – we form a society."

Rod pulled open the back door of the kitchen and peered out into the fog. After a moment, he closed it again and latched it tightly, setting the chain.

"Interesting perspective," said Jake. He dropped down to his knees and peered under the furniture and the appliances.

"Of course, to justify a system of laws, we made up gods. You can't have a believable system of justice that's not rooted in a god of some sort. That's what many of your new… say, what have you got there?"

"Looks like a peppermill," said Jake, holding a long ornate wooden rod that had been painstakingly turned on a lathe. It was clearly intended to make peppercorns into powder.

"Is that blood, there near the end?"

"Looks like it. Possibly some hair, also."

"Murder weapon?"

"That would be my guess. I suppose that you now agree that there's been a murder?"

"At the very least, someone got smacked very hard with a peppermill, and it wasn't anyone other than Ulysses, who is

48

apparently not present... So it's a reasonable inference that he's dead, by foul play. Or at least gravely injured."

"I'd agree," said Jake.

"You don't think that he crawled away somewhere, and is now languishing in some nook, in desperate need of prompt and urgent medical aid?"

"No, he was cold when I found him, and even if I was mistaken, he wouldn't have crawled away and taken all of his blood with him. There was a fair bit on the floor."

"Foul play, for certain, then," sighed Rod. "I suppose that we must update the others."

The group reassembled, without any instruction, in the parlor. They sank wearily into chairs and couches, with yawns and groans all around.

"No sign of him," said Nata.

"Us neither," said Ashton. Nata gritted her teeth, as if the ungrammatical nature of the phrase grated on her nerves.

"We did find this," said Rod, plonking the peppermill onto a low table that stretched in front of the couch. They all stared at it for a moment, before Nata spoke.

"The murder weapon?" she asked. "Is that blood?"

"We don't have a body," said Rod, "But we do have the evidence of a crime, and we have a missing person, Ulysses. We know he's not anywhere in the house. So the reasonable inference is that he's dead. Murdered."

"Killed with a peppermill," said Ashton. "God forbid."

"You mean, may chance forbid," snapped Marcion.

"May we not be so ill-fated," pronounced Guthrie.

"Not that we believe in fate," said Nata.

"So where do we go from here?" asked Ashton, sinking lower into his chair.

"I'd like a few hours of sleep," said Guthrie. "But with a murderer afoot, assuming there really is one, it hardly seems wise for any of us to nod off."

"We could nap for a while in these chairs, I suppose," said Nata. "Then we could set a guard."

"And if the guard is the murderer?" snapped Marcion.

"We could guard in pairs," said Rod. "Jake and I can take the first watch, then we'll wake Nata and Marcion in a couple of hours, and then Ashton and Guthrie can have a turn."

"Just like that, you've appointed us second watch?" sniffed Marcion. "As women, we must be harmless little servants? Up all night for the comfort of the men-folk?"

"Alright, will Guthrie and Ashton take the second watch?"

"Only if you'll shut up and let us get to sleep," said Guthrie.

"Should we take a moment to gather bedding from the rooms, before we settle down?" asked Nata.

The group looked at each other. "Can we declare a general truce? Perhaps agree that anyone who is being murdered will sing out loudly?" asked Guthrie. He staggered to his feet. "Back in a flash," he said, moving quickly toward the stairs.

"There will not literally be a burst of light on his return," said Ashton. "Do not expect to be enlightened in any way. I've known him twenty years, and there's no danger at all that he'll ever get any brighter than he is now."

The group, en masse, ascended the stairs, each stopping at a room, before emerging moments later and trouping back down to the parlor. Marcion threw together a nest of sorts upon a divan, while Nata carefully lined a davenport with proper sheets before applying a blanket and a quilt over the top of them. Guthrie threw a down comforter over a wingback chair near the fire, then sat on it and drew the ends around himself.

Ashton took another wingback chair, seating himself and then throwing a doubled-up quilt over top of him. He struggled with a pillow, trying to get it to stay behind his head without tilting him forward, and finally settled on wedging it in a corner and sliding down into the chair, which put more weight onto the pillow.

When they were snoring, each in a distinct tone, Rod turned to Jake. "Really," he said, in a soft voice, "I came to this event because I'd hoped for more discussion of the ethical dilemmas we all face as atheists. But none of these folks seem to really understand it."

"I'm sure that each has a reason for being an atheist."

"I'm not so sure. Remember what Tolstoy said about his own loss of faith – or that of the man who went hunting with his brother."

"Not sure that I recall the story."

"Oh, they're both in *My Confession*. For Tolstoy, someone simply told him that there was no God, and that was that. In the other story, the two brothers went on a hunting trip, and as they prepared to sleep, one of them started to pray. The other just said, 'Oh, you still do that?' and that single offhanded remark was enough to end his faith."

"It doesn't sound like a very solid faith."

"Quite nominal, apparently. So it was among the Tsarist-era Russian nobility. Christians in name only."

"A pity. Russia had been a Christian nation since 988. What is that? About nine hundred years by Tolstoy's time?"

"Curious that you should know that."

"Not really; it has to do with an obscure prayer ministry in which I was once involved."

"Well, my point being, of course, that these –" He gestured to the mounds of bedcoverings that surrounded them. "These are the same sorts of atheists, not for any real rational reason, but because their fragile little faith got knocked over. As a true rationalist atheist, it's always a bit insulting to me. As Marcion would say, it's a slap in the face."

"Can an atheist such as you call himself a rationalist?"

"What do you mean?"

"Well, you reject the idea of design, and you reject the idea of reason as the *Imago Dei*, so how can you rely upon reason?"

"A good question. Reason, as we perceive it, is merely a by-product, of course. We must have lucked into it."

"But that implies that there actually is some kind of an intentional end result, which would require design. Evolution is supposed to be a completely blind process: the simple result of those creatures which reproduce most, and thus are those which are best fitted to their environments, succeeding where other species die off."

"Well, we do sometimes see what we call evolutionary dead ends. The entire dinosaur thing, for example. Reason might be one more such dead end. It was something that seemed useful, and it was for a while, avoiding tigers and that sort of thing, but it just isn't as helpful now."

"But in actual experience, reason seems to be detrimental to keeping the species going over all. The most literate populations have the lowest rates of reproduction. And reason has given us things like the atomic bomb – the ability to not merely end a few populations, but possibly our entire species.

"Also, if the purpose of reason is to help us survive long enough to reproduce, how is it at all helpful that the human mind directs us to make beautiful paintings, to write long novels, and to compose symphonies? Or to search out the edges of the universe, knowing we'll never reach those distant stars? Or to discover mathematical oddities?" Jake raised his eyebrow to underscore his question.

"It is an unsolved question in evolution theory, how the advanced tiger-avoidance machines inside our skulls can give us things like calculus, I will have to grant you that. Pure science is a complete enigma to an evolutionist. But I'm sure that there is an answer, though science has not yet given it to us."

"I'll grant you both a crack in your skulls if you don't stop yammering," said Marcion. "We're trying to sleep over here."

Rod shrugged towards Jake, who drew out his pocket testament and began to read. In light of the discussion to date, the fifteenth chapter of 1st Corinthians seemed to be a very appropriate place to start. When he had read that, maybe Acts 17 would be a good follow-up passage, with Paul arguing against the pagan Greeks on Mars Hill.

Chapter Seven

JAKE AWOKE TO THE very pleasant odor of cooking food. It took him a moment to recognize the flavor, but it seemed to be a chicken linguini Alfredo... Or perhaps a Cacciatore? Those flavors were so unalike, and yet both so distinctly present, that he was left thoroughly baffled. It had to be one or the other. Yet it seemed that he smelled both.

And coffee. Yes, he was absolutely certain that he smelled fresh hot coffee.

He lifted one eyelid, and found himself in the great room, curled into an overstuffed chair, entangled with a blanket that somehow left the small of his back exposed to a draft. Opening the other eye, he saw Marcion, standing with arms crossed, staring into the dining room. Through the doorway, Rod and Nata were fussing with something on the dining table.

He straightened himself in the chair and regretted it at once. His joints made noises and sent twinges of pain and discomfort up his central nervous system. He was stiff and cold from his poor sleep. One of his calves felt like it was made of concrete.

The fire was roaring, so he got up and staggered over to it, regaining his sea legs and the circulation in his feet. The cold competed with the pins-and-needles sensations in his calves. He shifted his weight back and forth to better circulate the heat.

A quick survey of the room accounted for Ashton, who sat in his customary wingback chair, folding his quilt. Guthrie was nowhere to be seen. He looked at Ashton and caught his eye.

"Where's Guthrie?" he asked.

"Off killing Ulysses, no doubt," snapped Ashton.

"We should be keeping track of the group," said Jake.

"You Christians and your rules," snapped Ashton. "He went to the W.C., and no one needs to know what he's doing there. Or at least I don't."

"Point well taken," said Jake. "And as long as he's off by himself, he can't very well be murdered." He raised an eyebrow and cocked his head towards the dining room.

"Your two friends found some grub," said Ashton. "Some kind of victuals known as Em-Arr-Ease. They're preparing our breakfast, such as it will be. Never heard of this stuff, but it doesn't smell too bad."

"Meals, Ready to Eat," said Jake. "Shelf-stabilized food for long term storage. They must be mixing two different kinds."

"I wouldn't know. My only culinary talent lies in eating."

Guthrie came back into the room, drying his hands on a towel. "Whoever had next dibs, I'm back," he announced, sinking into the wingback opposite Ashton.

Nata chose that moment to step through the doorway. "Such as it is, breakfast is served." She pointed at one of the pots on the table. "Chicken Cacciatore is on the right, and linguini Alfredo with chicken is on the left."

"We used four servings of each," said Rod, entering the room. "Hopefully, between them, that will be enough. Also, there are all of the other things one finds in an MRE pack, like crackers, chocolates, condiments, that sort of thing."

"Coffee and fixings are on the side table," added Nata.

The other four shuffled into something resembling a line and began to meander towards the food. Jake yielded to the clearly-hungry Ashton, who tried to push his way past Marcion, but was rebuffed.

He had a package of crackers, a cup of coffee, and a bowl of the Cacciatore. It was a little odd to be eating dinner food for breakfast, but on the other hand, he doubted that there was any such thing as a breakfast MRE. Perhaps it was his hunger, but the meal seemed more than adequate, bordering on excellent.

Nata took a seat near him. "You'll be happy to know that I never allowed Rod of out my sight," she said, as she twirled a fork of linguini.

"Well, one way or another, we have all apparently survived the night intact," he replied.

"I was thinking about it as I slept." She dangled her tea bag up and down in the steaming teacup before her. "I mean, this entire issue of never being alone."

"And what did you conclude?" He carefully crumbled a pair of crackers into the remaining sauce in his bowl.

"We don't actually need to all stay together," said Nata. "One of us, wandering off alone, is in no danger, so long as the other five are in here."

"For that matter," said Rod, "Two might wander off singly, so long as the four are still in here. If one of them is killed, then the other must be the murderer."

"Not necessarily," said Jake. "Suppose that one of us – call her One – goes to answer the call of nature, and another of us decides to step out for some reason – maybe to have a quick smoke." He spooned the crackers Cacciatore from his bowl and ate them with relish.

"Filthy habit, that," said Ashton. "Putting burning leaves into one's mouth of one's own free will. Imagine."

"Call the second person Two," continued Jake. "Two returns shortly, while One is still away, and Three goes to get a drink of water. On his return, Four goes to answer nature, and immediately finds One dead. Was it Two, or was it Three who killed her?"

"Or even number Four?" asked Guthrie. "Or does the act of finding the victim seem a bit too cute?"

"It would be a risk, to say the least," said Rod. "But it would eliminate Five and Six from contention."

"Not necessarily. They might have made a murder trap," said Marcion. "Or there could be a conspiracy. Like the thing on that oriental train."

"Oriental train?" asked Rod.

"She's referring to Agatha Christie's *Murder on the Orient Express*. It was one of her Hercule Poirot stories. As it turned out, all of the suspects participated in the murder," said Jake. Marcion scowled at him, obviously adding knowing-what-she-meant to his growing list of crimes against humanity.

"Nonetheless," said Nata, "We could allow up to two individual excursions at a time, so long as each person checks in at the same time, and before a third is released."

"It's like one of those puzzles with the fox, the chicken, and the grain," said Jake. He looked at a sea of staring faces. "You know," he continued. "A man must cross a river with a fox, a chicken, and a large bag of grain. The canoe will only hold the man and one of the other items. Whichever he takes across leaves something in jeopardy – The chicken and fox can't be left together, nor the chicken and the grain."

"I'm not sure that riddles and word problems are what the world needs just now," said Guthrie. "I'd give my kingdom for a working cell phone."

"In most mystery novels," said Ashton, "The hero would rake the remains of those other cell phones from the ashes, and rebuild something… A telegraph, maybe."

The assembled group looked expectantly at Jake.

"I'm afraid that I'm rather useless with electronics," he said. "I can use them, but repair is out of my comfort zone."

"Don't keep us in suspense," said Nata. "What's the solution to the river problem?"

56

"Well, first he crosses with the chicken. The fox will not eat the grain, nor vice versa."

"Alright, but that's only one."

"Next he brings the fox, but he takes back the chicken. On the next trip, he brings the grain. Again, the fox will not eat the grain, so it's safe."

"Ah," said Rod. "Then one more trip to recover the chicken, and he has moved all three at no peril."

"What stops the fox from running away?" asked Ashton.

"He's an exceptionally well-trained fox," said Nata.

"But he couldn't be trained not to eat the chicken?" asked Guthrie. "Pfft."

"It's not the fox eating the chicken that the man is afraid of," said Nata. "The chicken is a psychopath, and has practiced Brazilian Jiu-Jitsu. He's afraid that the chicken will murder the fox. That's why the chicken is always alone."

Ashton opened his mouth to object, caught the twinkle in Nata's eye, and closed his trap. Guthrie rolled his eyes and tore open a large condiment package, conspicuously marked with MilSpec A-A-20328A. He squeezed the bottom of the pack and sucked out the peanut butter.

Marcion glared at him. "That's rude," she said.

"Now that we've solved the fox-and-chicken riddle," said Rod, "Perhaps we will wish to solve one of the real riddles before us. Such as how to get to the mainland."

"When the fog clears, we can try to signal someone on the bridge," said Nata.

"I think that there are some flares in a box under the stairs," said Guthrie. "You that actually have some skills, feel free to go and wave them about, fog or no fog. Use that remorse code, or whatever it's called."

"The sort of flare one shoots up into the sky?" asked Rod. "We might attract the Coast Guard."

"No," said Ashton. "The highway wreck sort of flare. What Canadians and Brits would call a fusee."

"Ah," said Rod. "The other sort would likely more readily be recognized as a distress signal."

"We could also work on the other problem at hand," said Nata. "Who killed Ulysses, that is."

"That's for the police to figure out," said Marcion. "Do you think that Father Blue over here is going to suddenly snatch an answer from the air? Quickly, there, Padre, step lively and point to someone. Say *J'accuse!* and show us the murderer."

"I'm afraid I can't do that just now," said Jake.

"We can hardly expect him to have solved the murder in his sleep," said Nata.

"Why not?" asked Guthrie. "He likely dreamed up the body to start with."

"Well, Ulysses *is* actually missing," said Rod, shrugging his shoulders. "Obviously something happened to him, and the idea that he was killed is as reasonable an inference as any other."

"Suppose Jake had solved it in his sleep anyway," said Nata. "To name a murderer now, when we have no way of arresting the accused, would merely make it imperative that the murderer kill all of the rest of us."

"And that would impair the murderer's ability to blend in with the innocents when the boat finally comes," said Jake.

"By the way, Jake," said Nata, "We probably should tell you: while you were sleeping, we voted to have you solve the murder for us."

"I'm flattered," said Jake. "But I'm not–"

"A policeman, or very much even of a logician," snapped Marcion. "You've got as much chance of figuring out the murder as you do of proving that your God is real."

"A good chance, then," said Jake. "So, since I'm under the gun here, I suppose we might begin by reciting where we were just before the body was discovered."

"I was sleeping soundly," said Guthrie. "Then came your ham-fisted drumming on the door. It was like something from Edgar Allen Poe. Pounding on my chamber door! A dimwit pastor, nothing more! Scared me half out of my wits! And then you demanded that we all come down here, and you won't let us go. Typical of you Christians."

Jake nodded and turned his face towards Ashton.

"I was visiting the W.C., as one my age is wont to do in the night." said Ashton. "I was on my way back to my room, and there you were, coming out of my room. As I explained to you at the time, if you will recall."

Jake turned to Marcion. "I was asleep," she said, in a weary tone. "And if I had my way, I'd still be."

"Quoth the raven," said Guthrie. "Or so it seems."

Nata spoke from the other side of Jake. "I know it must have been odd, finding me in a damp raincoat," she said. "I thought I heard a cat out the window, on the roof. It must have been scared by the storm. So I started to crawl out, but there was that light sprinkling rain–"

"More like a heavy mist," growled Ashton.

"Anyway, I put on the raincoat, and I had just stepped out the window when you knocked on the door."

"Did you find the cat?"

"No, and I very nearly lost my footing," she said. "If my reflexes were slower I'd have gone off, and all the way down the eastward cut. I shudder to think."

"The eastward cut?"

"This island was formerly mined for Manganese. The miners left the heavy equipment down by the dock – well, by where the dock is now. They also left a sharp cliff, and on one side of the building, this cliff – the eastward cut – is just outside the windows. Down below. I could easily have been killed."

"Jake may have saved your life," said Rod.

"He did that in high school," she replied. "And once is more than enough."

"That leaves me," said Rod. "I was sitting up reading. Petersen, *The Imago Dei as Human Identity*. It's still there, on the nightstand by the bed. I wanted to be able to take Jake to task over his views on this so-called *Imago Dei*."

"I'm flattered," said Jake.

"So now," asked Ashton, "What's your story, Jake?"

"I woke up, and it occurred to me that we might have been irresponsible with the cooking fires. I went to the kitchen to see if we'd left the ovens burning, and that's when I found the body. Ulysses, that is.

"I wasn't sure what to do about it – In my years as a pastor, this exact circumstance has never come up before. So I woke everyone, partly just to make sure that you were all still alive. Sounding the general alarm, so to speak."

"Why did you hide the body?" asked Guthrie.

"I didn't," said Jake. "I left it where I found it."

"A likely story," growled Marcion.

"It would have been foolish of me to find the body and then hide it again. And if I'd killed him, then doubly so. I'd have been better off just going back to bed and letting someone else find it later, when they went down to the kitchen for coffee."

"Just to play the *teufel-advokat*," said Rod, "If we take your story as given, then one of us was already down here, and moved the body after you discovered it, but before we returned with you. So, let us suppose, for a moment, that you killed Ulysses, then, hearing a sound and realizing that someone else was afoot, hid the body, lest the other person catch you *in flagrante delicto*.

"But you thought to yourself, what if you were seen out and about, by whoever was lurking – the person whom you heard – when you should have been upstairs, sound asleep? So you cleverly reported finding the body, in order to throw suspicion off of yourself."

"Very clever of me," said Jake, "And there's your proof: I'm not that clever."

"Well, of course you would say that," said Guthrie.

"We'll need to do a full background check on our next Jesuit," said Ashton. "We need to make absolutely sure that he's not clever like this one."

"I'm not a Jesuit," said Jake.

"See what I mean?" said Ashton.

"Did anyone else hear the cat outside?" asked Marcion, directing her glare against Nata. "This raincoat story of hers sounds a bit suspect. I've never seen a cat on this island."

"Never mind the cat. If Jake heard a thump down in the parlor, as he was about to climb the stairs, then there must have been someone in the parlor to make the noise. That goes without saying, of course," said Guthrie.

"And yet you said it," muttered Marcion.

"So how did that person get back upstairs and into his room? So that suggests that either there is a seventh person about, or…" Guthrie scanned their faces.

"Or what?" snapped Marcion.

"Or we have an unreliable narrator, who can't be trusted." Guthrie glared at Jake.

"Well, we also have Ashton, who was out of his room and very oddly dressed for sleeping," said Rod. "He might have come up the stairs after Jake did, and then blended in with the rest of us as we were coming from our rooms. His outfit for going to the loo is a bit strange."

"He was fully dressed, in fact," said Nata.

"Dressing to go to the 'loo is an odd, but honorable and ancient, military tradition," said Ashton.

"Be that as it may, we have no proof that you were upstairs at the time of the murder, or the time of the bodysnatching."

"I have a heart condition," said Ashton. "I wouldn't be able to carry a corpse around. You'd have found me passed out on the stairs, or else dead."

"Given his obvious weight and lack of physical fitness, we can take that for granted," muttered Marcion.

"He couldn't have hidden the body, but he might well have killed him," said Nata. "Do you have anything against Ulysses?"

"Aside from all of James Joyce's endless run-on sentences, not particularly," said Ashton.

"Gentlefolk," said Jake, "I am willing to stipulate, *ad hoc*, that Ashton is not the killer."

"What proof do you have?" asked Rod.

"I'm not willing to say just yet, but I have in mind a scenario that explains everything; however, that scenario makes it impossible for the killer to be Ashton. So, for now, until I'm able to test a couple of hypotheses, I'm considering him to be provisionally innocent, at least of this crime."

"Do me next," snarled Marcion. "Why couldn't I have done it? Am I just too nice a person to be considered?"

"One way to know that Ashton was innocent would be if you had done it yourself, Jacobs," said Guthrie. "And thus far, you've only denied moving the body. You did not deny killing him in the first place."

"I deny that as well."

"Well," said Marcion, "You've exonerated fully one third of the people here. Progress. Or complete and utter nonsense."

"I wonder if it would be possible to see Ulysses' room?"

"Well, if we had that servant here, we could allow him to let you in. But that's not going to happen."

"The doors don't lock on these rooms," said Guthrie. "But we've already checked the room last night, when we were trying to find him. Ashton and I, that is. Ashton, the exonerated."

"I'd like to have a peek anyway," said Jake. "Just to confirm a hypothesis, if you don't mind. Which room is his?"

"Above mine, in the attic. I suppose you'd call it a garret."

Jake rose from his chair. "I'll be back before you miss me."

Chapter Eight.

THE GARRET PROVED TO be a truly miniscule space, accessible only by a folding ladder attached to the trap door. Jake pulled the rope to lower the trap door, and then folded down the rickety wooden ladder. It moved and creaked as he ascended, and made him question whether he should have worked harder to control his weight.

Still, the ladder held up, and he moved up as quickly as he could, to get his weight off the ladder. In a moment he was in the garret, and in the dark. The light switch had to be near the ladder. He groped for it in vain.

He felt around over his head, in case it was on a pull-string, like old-fashioned garage lights. Nothing came within his grasp, so he felt to the wall again, and this time felt the switch, near his knee. He flicked the switch, and was rewarded by several bare bulbs coming to light.

The space was very small, about eight feet wide and twelve feet long. The floor was bare plywood, and the room was lined in sheetrock, taped but not mudded, or only lightly so. Screw holes and seams had a light skim of compound.

The light switch he had just found did not have a cover plate over it. He could see the wires in the box, behind the switch. He wasn't sure if that was okay, from a building safety perspective, but the building had stood this long, so he assumed that it was safe enough for the time being. Directly across from the switch, an electric outlet was also missing its plate.

Most of the space in the lower room of the attic was taken up by bare wooden shelves. They consisted of half-sheets of plywood nailed over a rough two-by-four frame. They were about right for boxes of accounting records. Obviously, this had been meant as a storage area, and not as sleeping quarters. For the most part, the shelves were barren, except for a fine coating of dust.

One of the top shelves had a stack of thin grey blankets, and one near waist high held a small and dusty stack of books, perhaps half a dozen in total. A particular book caught Jake's eye, or rather, two identical books: *Concentric Counterfeits*, by Carlisle Guthrie. Jake picked up one copy of the book and skimmed it. It seemed, at first blush, to be a slightly sensational book on the paranormal sites of ancient Britain.

It was hardbound, with cover jacket intact, and aside from dust, it looked like it had just come from the publisher. The edges of the pages crackled slightly as he flipped through them, as if the gilt edges had never been separated. Jake was obviously the first to open these pages. He turned to the back cover.

Was Stonehenge truly a druid holy place, or was it an early Victorian fraud, designed to bilk money from unwary tourists? Jake quickly concluded that Guthrie leaned towards the latter answer. It might be an interesting light read, maybe for a rainy afternoon, he supposed, but it was unlikely to help much now.

One of the other books was the memoirs of Dr. Rodel Dobrazamery, of the Reichenbach Falls Hospital, in Bohemia. This one, at least, showed a tiny bit of wear. The dust jacket was missing, but the spine still showed the same color as the front and back covers.

The other books in the stack were cookbooks. All of them were covered in dust, and they had not been recently disturbed.

He restacked them, as best he could. Besides the books, there were no other artifacts on this level.

It was an intriguing little library, but Jake supposed that it was customary to donate one's books to one's club, provided one had both a book and a club. He idly wondered if Nata had a book somewhere, but it seemed like a bad time for a scavenger hunt, so he continued his exploration.

A steep stairway, roughly made from cheap hardware-store lumber, crudely framed into shape and never finished, rose to a mezzanine over half of the lower space. The mezzanine, or maybe loft was a better word, was perhaps eight by seven, and featured an unfurled sleeping bag. From the style and the wear of the pale green fabric, Jake would have dated it around 1970.

Around the sleeping bag were various other items: A small pack, a dime-store electric lamp, a small stack of paperback pocket books, an empty aspirin bottle, a rocks glass with a toothbrush in it, a number of empty paper bags, several neatly folded changes of worn clothing, and a battered old manual typewriter. A page was curled round the platen, and had been about half-typed.

It was a scene from a romance novel, and it took about two lines to make Jake decide he'd rather be shot than to read the whole manuscript. Below the most recent paragraph, there were two blank lines, and then a single sentence: *Carthago Delenda Est.*

Jake looked around the scene a second time, taking in more detail. On top of the sleeping bag, there was a thin couch pillow wrapped in an old blue towel. The lamp was plugged in, and worked when Jake tried it, but the bulb was a bit dim, especially for reading. That fact drew his attention back to the stack of paperback books.

Ulysses must only have read in the daytime. Or maybe he only read down in the drawing room. That would explain many things about the bolt-hole he had made for himself in the garret.

If this were one of the Victorian mysteries of which his wife was so fond, there would be a book that Ulysses had left in the drawing room, and it would hold a vital clue to the name of his murderer. Jake made a mental note to inspect the drawing room at his first chance, just on the off chance.

Most of the books were random second-hand-store rejects, pocket size, with a couple of trade paperback size in the stack. They were shopworn and scratched-up, until all the bindings were broken and the pages were coming loose. One of the pocket books was by Dr. Elvirita-Anita Marcion, and bore the captivating title, *Why There is Very Obviously No God, and Shame on Him for That.*

Jake understood why she would not want to be called by her first name, under the circumstances. He made a note to research her book, once he was safely back on the mainland. He found himself idly wondering if it could possibly be as horrible as the title suggested.

Something was peeking from under the edge of the sleeping bag, near where a pillow would be if there were one, which there wasn't. With a pencil, Jake slid it out. It was a small flat bag, of the sort used by gift shops and stationers. Its red logo and caption advertised the Amazing Grace Elephant Shop, on Arsenal Road, Wan Chai, Hong Kong.

Inside was a gold watch. Flicking it open, he saw that the time had stopped at 9:48. Opposite the face, a photo had been cut down to fit inside. Two men in Vietnam-era army fatigues smiled at the camera. One of them looked like Ulysses, but was thinner and far younger. A hand-penciled caption on the back of the photo read, "Don't Mess With The Delta Dogs! Hoo-wah. 11-6-72."

Jake snapped the watch closed, slid it back inside the bag, and put it back under the sleeping bag. Nothing else in the room caught his eye, so he made his way down the steep wooden stairs, and then down the rickety folding stairs.

Nata was sitting on the next to the last step of the marble staircase, on the first floor. She stood up as he came by.

"Find anything?" she asked.

"Maybe," said Jake. "It's not always easy to tell."

"So what is she like?"

"Who?"

"This wife of yours. Bryly, I think you called her."

"Sweet, smart, and 40 weeks pregnant," he said. "Our first."

"Just a suggestion, but Illuminata is a lovely name."

"We're going with Faith, but the name Lisa did cross my mind. Partly in your memory."

"But you couldn't do it, because Bryly was dead-set against ex-girlfriends? Thou shalt have no lovers before me?"

"No, I think she'd have been fine with it. In the end, Faith just seemed like a more fitting name."

"We weren't exactly lovers anyway," she said. She took a step, and they strolled together into the parlor.

"It's about time!" shouted Marcion. She levered herself off of the sofa and started towards the stairs.

Bryly awakened a second time, and not for Faith's sake. She drew a deep breath and stretched her arms. Maybe the secret to getting good sleep was to sit in a chair. It seemed to work better for Faith, at least.

The room was now brightly lit, with sunlight streaming from every window. The small clock on the mantel claimed that it was nearly noon. She had trouble believing that.

She made her way upstairs to fetch her phone, in case Jake had called or texted while she was napping. It was a very slow process – Jake would have called it a laborious climb, and then would have dodged the pillow that she would have thrown at him for the pun.

There were no messages and no texts. Her heart sank. On the one hand, she didn't feel right to worry about him, but on the other hand… She frowned as she made her way back down the stairs again, for her coffee.

The coffee was in the coffeemaker, but was now cold. She poured a large mug and slid it into the microwave. She yawned, clicked two minutes, and listened to the oven humming.

She supposed some lunch might be in order, and for some reason, chicken cacciatore came to mind. It sounded really tasty right then. Maybe if Jake were there, she'd have tried to make some, but it seemed like too much work just for her. Or maybe that was just a weird pre-natal craving.

She could almost understand Jake not calling last night, she supposed. He might have arrived late, and felt very tired, or he might even have just forgotten. But him not calling or texting this morning, and not asking how little Faith was doing… That was unusual. He sometimes even called her from the office in the middle of the day, just to check in.

She wondered if she should call him – but what if he were in the middle of a speech? Or a presentation, or whatever it was that these OAR folks did. She'd feel silly to interrupt, and it would be rude to embarrass him in front of the group, just because she hadn't slept well without him. She was certain he'd call that evening.

The microwave bleeped, summoning her to her coffee.

"We had set the morning aside, on our schedule, for a little exercise called Freestyle Debate," said Ashton, rising from his seat. "But that's been shot all to hyperbole."

"We wasted the entire morning chasing Ulysses," growled Guthrie. "He's probably up a tree somewhere, waiting to be rescued." He raised a spoon of Beef Stroganoff *a-le-M.R.E.*, and stared at it as though it had teeth.

"So this afternoon, then, was meant to be a lecture by Dr. Marcion. *Offensive Bible Passages* was the topic, I believe. Once we've finished this light lunch, of course." He lowered himself back into his chair and tore open a packet of instant potato flakes, to which he added hot water from a cup at his left elbow.

"Light lunch? This is more of a slight lunch. You simply cannot truly expect me to speak after this sorry excuse for a meal," said Marcion. "It's like having no nourishment at all. Actually, no nourishment at all would be better, because this is an insult; it's a slap in the face. I simply shall not be able to speak. My mental processes have been stultified by starvation. Not that you'd learn anything anyway, as dense as the lot of you seem to be. I'd be better off talking to myself." She bit into a soup cracker with suppressed fury.

"It has been a stressful forenoon," said Nata. "Perhaps we should forgo the schedule altogether, and concentrate on just staying alive until we're rescued."

"I'd still like to hold the Freestyle Debate," said Marcion. "We've had no chance yet to grill this sorry excuse for a Jesuit. His religion must pay for its sins."

"Jake has done, and is doing, a very valuable service for us all," said Nata. "On top of that, he's been very gracious. Grilling him on your favorite internet memes would be very ungracious. And ungrateful."

"Next you'll want to sign him up for full membership in our organization," said Guthrie. "No doubt, you'll also want to knock off fifteen-percent as a friends-and-family discount."

"That might not be a bad idea," said Rod, gesturing with his spoon. "It just might improve the general level of dialog around here. He's quite clever, fast on his feet, and has a philosophical position that is capable of being rationally defended."

"Oh, not the old Rome-and-Carthage routine again, please, please," muttered Marcion. "Will someone fetch the peppermill now and relieve me of my pain?"

"That depends on your definition of rational," said Ashton. "I'm sure that his entire defense consists of quoting all the right bible verses. God is obviously real, because the bible tells us so. That's what they all do, when cornered."

"In light of our present predicament," said Nata, "Instead of attacking Jake, shouldn't we all be working on some way to summon rescue?"

"Defending him again? Just whose side are you really on?" snapped Marcion.

"Who says we need rescuing?" asked Guthrie. "I can't speak for the lot of you, but I've got a warm fire here to sit by, and something vaguely resembling food. In a pinch I could find a book to read."

"And whistle up a murderer," said Nata.

"Or as they call them in Canada, National Health workers," said Rod. He paused for the expected laugh, which did not come forth. "I do suppose that's a bit unfair," he conceded, after an awkward moment.

"It does raise a philosophical point," said Jake. "Suppose that a person has suffered a painful and life-changing injury. Suppose that a doctor has an opportunity to discreetly end the patient's life, with no suspicion and no repercussions. We'll assume it's a country without any kind of assisted suicide laws. Ought the doctor, of his own volition, to do so?"

"How painful?" asked Ashton.

"Whatever level of ongoing pain you believe would justify whatever actions you recommend," said Jake. "But is that the watershed, then? The actual degree of the pain? Or perhaps the degree of ongoing disability?"

"You're trying to get us onto a slippery slope argument, is that it, Jacobs? It won't work." Marcion crossed her arms and scowled at him.

"You won't find a hospital in Carthage," said Rod. "That's an invention of you Christian Romans, with your *Imago Dei*. For that matter, there were none in Rome until you Christians took over. And I see right through your trick. David Hume to the rescue: One cannot derive an ought-statement from any number of is-statements." He smirked.

"Alright, you've made the point," said Guthrie, with a sigh. "I give in. It's better to be rescued than to listen to this drivel."

The phone rang. It took Bryly a moment to realize that it was her phone, and another to realize that she needed to answer it. Shaking the cobwebs from her mind, she glanced at the screen. It wasn't Jake.

"Hello," she answered, trying to sound cheerful.

"Bryly, hi, is Jake there?"

She recognized the voice of Reynaldo, one of the deacons.

"No, Rey, he's away at that meeting, up in the bay, until sometime tomorrow. I had expected him to call last night, but I

70

guess he got busy with his speech and everything." She hoped the fear in her mind didn't filter through to her voice.

"Yeah, I've already tried his cell phone a couple of times. It went straight to voicemail. If you do get through to him, could you have him call me? Or Deacon Nguyen, either one."

"Anything I can do?"

"Well, not unless you know where the circuit breakers are for the baptistry water heater. We're going to baptize Byron this Sunday, you know. I came down to make sure that the heater worked and that the pipes were rinsed out, but we can't get any hot water out of this thing."

"I hope we don't have to baptize him cold."

"Us, too. It's a bit too much of an ordeal to make a convert go through, just to join a church. Kind of a polar plunge. Hey, I think maybe Chi Due found something. Gotta go." He hung up.

She stared at the phone in her hand for a moment. Then she glanced at the cup of coffee, barely started, on the small table beside her chair. She sipped it, and as she suspected, it was cold. She put it down.

Maybe she and Faith would get by without it, she decided. She rose from the chair with considerable effort, and toddled into the kitchen in search of a healthful, if slightly late, lunch. As an afterthought, she made her way back into the living room and picked up her phone.

Jake's phone rang twice – it takes that long for the carrier to find the phone, she knew. Then his cheerful voice asked her to please leave a name and a number. "Euphonia Evertrue," she said. "Seventy-one."

Jake would understand. She hung up.

Nata set the large cardboard box of fusees next to the bare patch of ground, from which Rod had carefully scraped away the dry grass with a shovel. Dry grass might not have been the right term: Dead and once dried, but now damp from dew, however, was far too clumsy a descriptor. The moisture seemed to give it a strong hay aroma.

71

She arranged the flares in a snake pattern, each resting at the base of its predecessor, with the striking end exposed. On the far end of each, the tab of the small plastic lid kept the flare from rolling down. With a bit of geometric creativity, she made the zig-zag turn a corner, and then run parallel to itself, ending near where it started. She looked up to Rod.

"Well, that's ten of them – eleven if I strike this one to light those. Will that be enough?"

"According to the box label, they're rated for twenty minutes. If we take off about twenty percent for inefficiency and wishful thinking, that's 160 minutes." He glanced at a wristwatch. "Call it two and a half hours?"

She looked up at the bridge. She could almost make out its shape through the fog, but she couldn't see any lights at all. Perhaps it was just the dim daylight, or perhaps drivers weren't using their headlights. In this fog, she didn't see how they could avoid it. The visibility was nearly nothing.

"Here we go," she said, striking an eleventh fusee and then holding it on the striking end of the first flare in the long chain. "Hopefully someone will see it."

When the first one in the chain flared, she laid the lit fusee beside its colleagues, and followed Rod back into the house.

Ashton and Guthrie had set up a chess board, and were working on a game. Guthrie appeared to be asleep, his hooded lids hiding the tiny sliver of his eyes. Ashton, by contrast, seemed nearly apoplectic. Marcion sat nearby, watching and scowling at the board, or perhaps merely at the idea of chess.

Nata glanced at the board as she passed by. Ashton seemed to be trying to work a Ruy Lopez with the white pieces against Guthrie's Guicco Piano. She shook her head. That was unlikely to work out well for Ashton.

"You don't approve?" said Rod, in an undertone.

"Black should play a defense, not an attack. The Sicilian would be my recommendation. Or a King's Indian."

"You play?"

"Somewhat," she confessed. "My FIDE rating, if I played regularly, might be around 1750 or so. Possibly 1800 if I worked at it for a while."

"Ah, yes. Jake mentioned that you were in the chess club together. So I presume that he plays as well."

"It wasn't a true chess club per se. It was more a group of students, to whom a teacher would open his classroom at lunch. Chess sets and backgammon were simply provided for whoever wanted to play. There was no real attendance, there were no meetings, and we never did any of the normal activities as a club. Like going to exhibitions, things like that. We just played chess. Sometimes backgammon or acey-deucey."

"As an anarchist at heart, I approve of this informal club. And your Jake, he had some considerable skill, did he not?"

"I don't know why you guessed that, but, yes, he was known for his imaginative positions. Never quite the textbook move. It was impossible to guess what he was thinking until the trap was sprung. If you were a book player, he'd send the game into the weeds and ambush you there."

"A student of the art from a young age?"

"More of a natural talent. The first time I saw him play, it was an utter slaughter. Humiliating. He was so terrible. But by the end of that year, he was the player to beat. I'm not sure when it changed. We started teaming up against him, giving him half our time, things like that."

"Blitz, then? He was a blitz player?"

"Well, it didn't work out that way. The time thing was a big mistake. We'd be whispering plans between ourselves while he was staring at the board, waiting. So, of course, once we finally moved a piece, he had an instant response. It was intimidating."

"He did his thinking on your time."

"Exactly. And the more he did that, the worse it got for us. We couldn't think on his time, because he was using ours. We finally snuck in a ringer to try to beat him — a highly ranked chess player from another nearby school. Rudy somebody. I don't recall his last name. But even that didn't work."

"Jake was that good?"

"He was lucky. Very lucky. Or good, maybe. He might have planned it all unconsciously, and then it just worked... It's hard to say. He made a Queen's Indian defense, and had all his pieces devoted to protecting the king, but Rudy was brutal. He just kept chiseling away at the fortification, taking one pawn at a time. All eyes were on the crumbling castle, eagerly awaiting its collapse.

"Suddenly, Jake withdrew one of his rooks to an open file. That practically gave away a bishop. Rudy just shook his head and captured it. But Jake pushed the rook up the open file, and it was checkmate. Out of the clear blue sky."

"Out of the clear blue sky, you say. No one saw it coming, no warning at all, then."

"No warning at all. He just slid the rook, and then he didn't even swagger. Just, 'Check, and I believe that's mate.'

"With hindsight, we should have seen it, too, I suppose. Or at least wondered what he was up to. I learned a valuable lesson: When someone does something you don't understand, ask yourself why. Part of my minor in psych was because of Jake."

"Intriguing that you still remember that game, after all these years. It must have made quite an impression on you."

"It did. I remember the moment when his brow suddenly smoothed out. He had been very intense, and then he got an odd look of utter confidence, calmly pulling the rook from the fray. But none of us saw it coming at all. We were focused on what Rudy was doing."

"And so, in the next move, with all of your eyes on the wrong part of the board, he took advantage of the timing – the initiative – to spring his trap? Like a magic trick?"

"Yes, the sacrifice of the bishop, completely unexpected – I guess it was really a gambit – allowed him to win the game."

"So we may expect him to suddenly accuse the murderer, without warning? When the killer thinks he is perfectly safe, a cold hand will descend upon his shoulder?"

"Maybe. He might be about to do a Sherlock Holmes, any second. Or he might still be fishing for the first clue right now. We'll never know until we all know."

"You clearly think highly of him."

"Yes. Once even more than now. But time passes."

"That could be an epitaph: But time passes."

"It can be mine, when the time comes."

"If you will excuse me, while everyone is in sight except Jake, I fear I must step away for a moment."

"It should be safe. Jake would never kill anyone."

"And I will promise in my turn not to kill him." He winked, and vanished up the stairs.

Jake appeared, only a few minutes later, unharmed. He was out of breath, and sank into a sofa to Nata's right. She got up and moved to the sofa.

"And where have you been, pray tell?"

"Wandered down to that eastward cut." He paused for a couple of breaths. "The way back up the hill is steeper than it looks. Much steeper."

"You're not quite as athletic as you were fifteen years ago," she said. "If I can be frank with you. Neither am I."

"You're not exactly telling me anything that my doctor hasn't already remarked on. And I forgave him, so..."

"I am gratified to have that same grace," she said. "But why did you go all the way down the hill?"

"Well, I had hoped that the miners had left some way to communicate. Maybe an abandoned telephone line."

"How would it stretch across from the mainland?"

"I hadn't worked that out. I suppose there would have to be some sort of an underground cable. Or underwater, across the channel to Richmond."

"And you found?"

"What the little boy shot at. Nothing."

"Naturally. No such luck. The fog normally burns off by now, though it hasn't yet. And eventually, the weather's got to improve. Who knows? Maybe someone has already seen our flares. Fusees. Whatever they're called."

"We can only hope." He finally brought his breath under control. "I suppose that eventually our loved ones will report us missing, and we'll be traced to this rock."

"Quite a few assumptions there, Jake. For example, that the authorities could know where we are."

"I assume that this island is listed among OAR's assets."

"One might be a bit hasty in making such an assumption. The legal circumstances of our presence are a bit, well, foggy. One might be forgiven for having the impression that we're mere squatters here."

"So this address isn't listed in any OAR literature?"

"Someone looking for our home office will likely trace it to a closed-up storefront on Oakland's High Street, or else a small room above Guthrie's garage, nearly Berkeley."

Jake chuckled. "I'm never going to let Father Somers forget this," he said. "I've apparently gotten him out of a lot more than just a speech and some heckling."

"Marooned," she said. "He's left you shipwrecked. Like the apostle Paul."

"But with fewer poisonous snakes."

"Marcion might leave a nasty bite," she said. "But even her venom seems pretty watery. And snakes or not, he did leave you in mortal danger."

"So far, the lot of you haven't dragged me out and stoned me to death, like the Apostle Paul at Derbe."

"I thought he got back up and went back into town after that. It was always a major preaching point, as I recall."

"His attackers thought he was dead. And before he got up, the church leaders surrounded him and prayed. It might have been a miracle. Luke doesn't say."

"We would certainly need a miracle to get us off this rock. No one even knows that we're out here."

"I'm sure the authorities will track us down. Someone will know that we met a bus at the train, and a boat at the pier. All we need to do is to wait for our loved ones to report us missing. MREs aren't great, but they'll get us through."

"That's another hasty assumption, Jake," she said, with a sigh and a wry smile. "You're assuming that there's anyone in this world who loves us."

Chapter Nine

TWO-THIRTY THAT AFTERNOON found Bryly with her nose in a book. She was about a third of the way through it, and was truly wishing that the author – some Troglodyte named Og Keep – would come to a point.

She grimaced. Maybe she was being unfair, and the fault lay in her own unease. She had left several messages for Jake. She was now up to Hortensia Happenstance, and the last number had been Seventy-four. She had also left several texts.

The next number she left would be 2.71828, so Jake would know that she realized how irrational she was being. That did nothing to calm her concerns, however. She had prayed for him; that should be enough to set her at ease. But still, she found herself worried that he was in mortal danger. It made it difficult to read, to knit, or to smite infidels on the internet.

That last pastime was made more difficult because the most recent group of atheists she had encountered had all gone silent. It was as if their internet connection had been severed.

Bryly tried reaching the OAR through their 800 number, but it had apparently been turned off. The more pedestrian phone number, in the 510 area code, east bay, announced that the principals of the organization were away at their annual retreat, in an undisclosed location.

Further digging revealed that the club was founded in 1911 to prevent the further promulgation of Christianity. That was more than a little troubling. Obviously, Jake had been lured there under false pretenses. Were they plotting his murder? Maybe that was how they worked to prevent the spread of Christianity: By killing off Christian pastors.

As she thought about that, it seemed indescribably silly. Jake would be back in a few short hours – twenty hours, maybe, give or take? – and he'd have a funny story to tell, about how his phone fell off the boat and was seized by seagulls. Or was eaten by a sea lion, or something equally silly and mundane.

Or it had fallen between the cars of the train and been run over. Whatever had happened, there would be a reason for it all, and she'd feel so silly that she'd beg him to delete all the text messages and voicemails.

Even as she thought that, she dialed him again. "Iona Isengard," she said, when Jake's voice asked her for a name and a number. "Pi." She hung up. She was not rational at all.

She could only think of one deacon's wife who was likely to be available during the day, so she called Nguyen Thao Trang. She answered on the first ring.

"Hello, Bryly," she said. "Thanks for calling back, but I think Chi Due and Reynaldo figured it out. There is a breaker panel on the roof, and that is where they found it. The water is getting hot now. Can you believe that? On the roof?"

"I can't imagine," said Bryly, and that was true. She had only the vaguest idea of what a breaker panel looked like, and none of how they worked. She definitely didn't know how one might be on a roof. Weren't they usually in basements?

"Yes, it was against the back wall of the sanctuary, up on the flat part that surrounds the steep part. Chi Due spotted it."

"Good eyes. I'm glad that's settled. I was actually calling you for another reason, though. Jake didn't call home last night. Normally he calls when he's away."

"Maybe he's too busy. Maybe there're no breaks at that conference he went to. There could be a lot of reasons. Some people are just work, work, work."

"Jake would have called this morning, at least. It's kind of silly, but I'm starting to worry about him."

"Of course you do. You're still newlyweds. When I first married Chi Due, often he would go on the boat and I would worry about sharks, or pirates, or an accident with those sharp knives they have. It was always for nothing."

"But I suppose there may be a good reason to worry about Jake. Have you tried calling the hospitals?"

"Well, but which ones? I did see him get onto the train, so I know he got that far, but..."

"I haven't seen any reports of a train wreck. We would have heard, it would have been big news. Where was he going? To what station?"

"Emeryville, in the East Bay."

"Maybe start with Emeryville police?"

"I'd feel silly if it were nothing."

"You'd feel horrible if it were something. What harm can a couple of little phone calls cause?"

"I suppose you're right. I'll give it a little more time, then I'll start making calls."

"Call me any time," said Thao Trang. "I will tell Chi Due, in case you need to go to the bay area."

"That probably won't be necessary."

"We are here to help."

As she disconnected, Bryly looked around the room. The house was quiet, eerily so. She dialed Jake's number once again. "Kordelia Kwartermain," she said.

"What about Ima Gine?" asked Jake.

"She has no time for her crazy old mother. She doesn't like any of the things I like, and she's in complete rebellion. Some of her friends — Honestly, Jake, this will sound very silly, especially to you, but I think they just might be sneaking down to the cathedral at night and lighting candles. Last week, I found a rosary under her bed."

"Oh, the horror," said Jake.

"I'm serious," said Nata. "I mean not that she might try to become a Christian or something; she can learn about it the same way I did. But it's the rebellion, the sneaking around. I don't know what to do with her."

"Kids can be difficult."

"You'll know all about that in a few years." Nata sighed. "It was different when she was small. When she needed me. Now I feel like – I don't know. I'm kind of adrift."

"You have to build bridges with your kids. You have to set up the common ground."

"HAH!" yelled Ashton, upsetting the board. The chess pieces rolled around the floor. The black king bounced off of an ottoman and landed at Nata's feet. She picked it up.

"I don't suppose you'd be up for a match?" she asked. In answer, Jake recovered the board and picked up the scattered pieces. He began finding each piece its proper place.

By the time Rod returned to the parlor, Jake had taken a King's Indian defense against Nata's Cramling Cow. No pieces had been taken as yet.

Rod watched a moment, then moved over near Ashton and Guthrie, who were debating in undertones, through clenched teeth, over the legality of touch-move in non-blitz chess matches. This move of Rod's apparently placed him too near Marcion, who got up from her seat and stormed off into the hallway. Her shoes could be heard clicking as she ascended the marble steps.

The cow opening that Nata was using – a relatively new chess opening, which Jake had never before seen – gained a little bit of footing at first, setting up a diagonal line of opposing pawns across center. With very little development towards center, it seemed to be an unusual, but potentially powerful, opening. Jake's Indian was as old as the game itself, or so the masters claimed, but it was hard to assault.

"When is the baby due?" asked Nata. She tapped her finger against a knight, then repositioned her queen's bishop. It might have been a ploy to disrupt his thinking.

"Well, if we've got the math right, about two or three weeks." He moved his knight into the fifth rank, but it didn't appear to pose a serious threat. "I really shouldn't be away like this – if I had known the island would be so isolated..."

"Or that Marcion would destroy all the usable cell phones on the island," said Nata.

"Right, that also. I wonder..." He waved his hand over his rook, decided against it, and lowered his hand again. Then, from nowhere, he pushed a pawn.

Both stared at the board in silence. Nata tried to guess, from the movement of his eyes, what he might be intending. She moved her queen to support a bishop.

Her analysis was in vain. Jake didn't actually have a plan for moving the game forward. He was merely "playing position," as his friends had called it in high school: Choosing the best move for the current state of the game, as if it were a puzzle in a magazine. It was seldom a winning method.

On the general principle of controlling center, he moved his other knight to attack a pawn, but the diagonal line of Nata's pawns would keep him from taking it freely.

"Are you happy, Jake?" she asked.

"Well, it's probably not my best move."

"Not in the game, or even here on the island. With life in general. With the way things are going."

"I suppose," he said. "I'm doing work I enjoy, I have a happy family, and I'm waiting on pins and needles to finally meet Faith. As you must have been once, with Ima Gine."

"That was then," she sighed, moving a pawn.

"I'm not qualified to give advice on this sort of thing, but there is a poster in Bryly's office. It goes, 'If you like how things are going, keep doing what you're doing. If you don't, change something.' Well, that strikes me as a good place to start."

"Easier said than done," said Nata, raising her eyes from the board and staring into his. "The problem is, what if I change the wrong thing and make it worse? Or what if I can't find the thing to change that makes it better?"

She looked back down and took a pawn, triggering an exchange on the queen's side. When the smoke cleared, Jake's knights were dominating center, but Nata's bishops were posed to make a serious threat against his fianchetto.

"I'm off to the 'loo," announced Ashton, struggling to his feet. "I trust that none of you will kill each other in my brief absence?" Jake scanned the room. Only Marcion was missing, so Ashton should be safe enough.

When he was gone, Guthrie turned his eye to the chess match. "Do you really have the time to be doing that? We're paying you to solve this alleged murder."

"No, you're not," said Jake. "That would be a violation of the professions code, since I'm not a private investigator." He moved a pawn, hoping Nata would take it, thus giving him access to her rook.

Nata ignored it, sliding her rook to an open file.

"Just like a Jes— Just like a Christian to slack off on the job," said Guthrie.

"Give it a rest," said Rod. He produced a magazine from somewhere, and began to thumb through it.

"I don't see this going well for me," said Nata. "If I'm reading this right, you're about three moves from a checkmate." She set her fingernail against the king's cross.

"Before you do that," said Jake, "Even if I did trade queens, as you're thinking, you'd still have an out. See, A2 puts you in the notch between those two pawns. And I have no bishops to close that diagonal."

She turned her eye, as he had hoped, to the knights. Her rook slid up the open file and stopped adjacent to one of them. It was merely harassment, easily dodged, but if she worked with her bishops, she might have something.

Guthrie coughed. It turned into a spasm. "I'm stepping out for a cigarette," he said, getting his feet under him and making for the French doors.

"There are already two people unaccounted," said Rod.

"Who appointed you to be our policeman?" asked Guthrie, without pausing.

A trade began in center, effectively reducing the board to pawns. Jake's three were in a chevron, in front of the king. Nata had a passed pawn on the queen's side, at the fifth rank. She pushed it forward.

Jake would not be able to get his king in front of it in time, so he moved the rook's pawn up two squares. Nata pressed into the seventh rank, her new queen imminent.

Ashton walked into the room and looked around. He scowled. "Where is everyone?"

"Guthrie stepped out for a cigarette, and Marcion appears to have gone to the 'loo," said Rod.

"Thought we were going two at a time. Safety in the math, saving the fox from the kungfu chicken."

"Guthrie had other ideas," said Rod. "But now that you mention it, kung pao chicken would be a tasty dinner."

"I'll phone out for delivery," said Ashton.

"Marcion's been gone a long time," said Nata. "I should go check on her."

"I'm in a badly losing position for black anyway," said Jake, knocking over his king.

Nata rose, and walked up the stairs. Almost at the same time, Guthrie let himself in through the French doors. He spotted Ashton at once.

"Chess?" he asked, winking at Ashton. Ashton growled.

There was a bit of shouting upstairs, followed by steps upon the staircase. Marcion, her clothes rumpled, stormed into the parlor. She looked like a cat that had lost a water-balloon fight, except that she was dry. Jake almost expected her to hiss at them and try to scratch.

"Can't even get in a quick nap," she snarled.

"Sorry," said Nata, who came in behind her. "I didn't mean to startle you. You'd been gone quite a long while, and we were starting to get concerned."

"Oh, I'm sure you were."

"Since it looks like we're all here - Rod, it's about time to add some more flares, I think."

"Why don't you take your old flame?" snapped Marcion. "I'm sure that the two of you just want time alone."

"I'm married," protested Jake.

"And that would stop you from lighting flares?"

"No, but I resent your implication."

"I resent your existence," she snapped, "But it doesn't stop me from doing my duties."

"Come on, Jake, go with me," said Nata. "She probably didn't realize how it sounded, and we'll be back before anyone can make up any rumors about us."

Jake allowed himself to be dragged out the French doors.

They returned a moment later. Drinks had apparently been served, and Rod was bending Guthrie's ear.

"Oh, come now," he was saying. "You can't just wave an as-yet-unknown law of nature in the air and claim that it's the cause of moral obligation. And that's assuming that we accept your premise that Buddhism is not actually a religion, but merely a philosophy."

"Is it impossible that there is an as-yet-unknown physical law?" demanded Guthrie.

"One that confers moral obligation? Yes, without a doubt. You should know that from Hume's famous is-ought problem."

"You're back quickly," said Ashton. "Forget something?"

"The flares are gone," said Jake.

"You've mislaid the box?" asked Marcion. "Well, ask Rod what fool thing it was that you fools did with them."

"No," said Nata, "They're not mislaid. I know precisely where we left the carton: It was under a certain scrub sagebrush with a blue nylon tarp wrapped around it. It was no more than a yard from the spot we scraped. It's not there."

"Well, there are bound to be more around," said Guthrie. "Go look in the closets, where you found the first carton. Not that they're particularly effective. We still haven't been rescued."

"You're missing the point," said Jake. "Not only is the carton gone, but so are the flares that Nata and Rod lit earlier. Not a trace left."

"Well, they obviously burned up," said Marcion.

"They'd have left ash, and chunks of burnt strontium," said Jake. "There's no trace of them. Not even the little plastic caps that keep them from rolling."

"Impossible," said Rod.

"But true," said Nata. "Someone must have gone back and snuffed the ones we lit, then disposed of all the rest."

"How?" snapped Marcion. "We've all been here, in this little room, this entire afternoon."

"Not all," said Rod. "We've each had a chance to step out for a moment or two, here or there."

"Let me propose a theory," said Ashton. "There's a man out there – maybe a homeless man who paddled across from Richmond in a crude raft. He snuck in last night, killed Ulysses, ate the eighth pie, and then stole Ulysses' body. He's camped somewhere by the manganese mine, and he stole the flares to use to cook the main course of last night's dinner. Which he also stole, of course."

"Should I point out the needless entities?" asked Rod.

"Here's a better theory," said Marcion. "These two didn't light any flares at all." She gestured to Rod and Nata. "Instead they went out and stared at the stars, to make that one jealous." She pointed to Jake.

"There weren't any stars," said Rod. "Just daylight and fog."

"The theory is still sound."

"It does require fewer entities, but I will swear to you that we lit the flares. I am sure that Nata will do likewise."

"By whom will you swear?" asked Guthrie. "By some god in whom we don't believe? Or by your own flesh?"

"I will affirm, then," he said. "Nata?"

"I also so affirm," she said.

"Take that or leave it," said Rod. "It's the best we can do."

"It would be nice if we could at least eliminate someone," said Nata. "But we've all been out alone for at least a few minutes. Time enough."

"I'll refresh drinks, if anyone's inclined," said Rod.

"Do we have any strychnine?" asked Marcion. "It would be an improvement over arguing about whether Buddhists can be atheists." She shook her head.

"I was thinking that we might stick to the more potable tinctures," said Rod.

"Whiskey again, then," she said.

"Gin and tonic," said Guthrie.

"White wine if we have it," said Nata.

"Do allow me to help," said Jake.

Rod shrugged, and the two men stepped into the kitchen.

"What was that about atheists and Buddhists?" asked Jake. "It sounded a bit bizarre."

"Oh, it was," said Rod, uncapping the open bottle of whiskey and splashing two fingers into a rocks glass. "Guthrie was trying to preserve moral imperative and still deny any kind of gods. He's not the first to go that way. I've had quasi-atheists like these claim that Taoism is not a religion, or pantheism as a whole, Confucianism, and now Buddhism. A desperate ploy."

"I can imagine," he said, pouring Nata's white wine. "It does seem as if atheists want to believe in something, but just not the Christian God."

"Those are fake atheists," said Rod. "A true atheist faces the world as the stark and comfortless thing that it is. They don't try to hide behind some neutered version of a religion." He chuckled. "It's a matter of time until they say that Islam is not a religion. I can't wait for that one."

"And the undiscovered law of nature?"

"A new wrinkle, I'll give him that," said Rod, adding a jigger of tonic to a generous shot of gin. "He first claims an atheistic Buddhism, so that the universe is like a god, but not really; then he postulates a law of nature, meaning a rule of the god that isn't a god, such that there is then a moral imperative."

"That sounds like doubletalk."

"It is. It's just meaningless babble. And of course he won't defend it in the slightest. It's a classic *Magister Dixit* ploy. He just keeps repeating it like a self-evident dictum from on high, and berating me for not 'getting it.' I ask you."

"Truly askew," said Jake.

"It's a common enough thing though; rejecting religion, and especially Christianity, on the grounds that it is a superstition, and then adopting some other superstition. I wouldn't be surprised in the least if Guthrie were to tell us a ghost story."

"He doesn't seem the type."

"They never do, until they do. Or take that old flame of yours. You noticed, no doubt, her jewelry?"

"The pendant and the two bracelets?"

"Did you recognize the stones? Moonstone on the pendant; to draw one's soulmate. Rose quartz on the left wrist; a sinister omen indeed. And Aventurine on the right: Two quartz' that remove bad will and foster communication between lovers, if the crystal-mongers are to be believed. She's merely replaced one superstition with another."

"Maybe she just thinks they're pretty."

"Are you willing to make a small wager on that point?"

Jake thought for a moment, then shook his head. He wasn't quite that certain. They picked up the glasses and headed back into the parlor.

Guthrie received his drink with stoicism, Nata hers with a smile, and Marcion hers with a scowl.

"There's too much soda in this," she protested.

"I didn't add any," said Rod.

She muttered about the poor quality of the whiskey, and retreated to her divan. She scowled at Ashton, not out of any ill will, but simply because he happened to be in front of her.

"I suppose we should give some thought to supper," said Nata, to Rod and Jake.

"We could simply let them all drink themselves into a coma, and then order out for pizza," suggested Rod.

"In addition to being cynical, that's impractical," said Jake.

"You're right, of course," said Rod. "We have no way to order the pizza."

"Pundora Persephone Peterson," said Bryly. She hung up the phone. That was the twelfth call Jake had missed. Her mind was full of things that might have happened to him. It was time.

Even though she dialed the non-emergency number, the Emeryville police took the call on the second ring. The report was routine, and the officer who took the call was professional, but mere routine did not comfort Bryly in the least. She had hoped, perhaps irrationally, for a huge cross-agency alert.

She didn't feel eating, but she had a nutrient milkshake, for Faith's sake. Then she made a large cup of a supposedly calming tea – "Awesome, Terrific, and Sweetly Soporific," as it styled itself. She thumbed through her stack of books to be read, but none of them really appealed to her in the moment.

There was a murder mystery from the perspective of a fish, called *A Diet of Worms*, but it didn't appeal to her. Too cold, too wet, and far too fishy.

She finally settled on a children's book about a moose who found a nativity scene, and imagined herself reading it to Faith. She could read it to her in reality soon enough, and that idea gave her spirits a small boost.

The rain began again.

Chapter Ten

"SHOULD WE ASSUME," ASKED Guthrie, through a fork wrapped tightly with spaghetti, "That whoever stole all of the flares is also the murderer?"

"It's not necessarily true," said Jake. "Someone might have a perfectly innocent reason for preferring our company here over returning to the mainland."

"If anyone does, let him or her speak up now," said Nata. "There will be no recriminations of any kind."

"Ha," said Marcion. "You're the only one with any reason to want us here. A bit self-serving to promise that there will be no recriminations, isn't it?"

"The issue will be resolved soon enough," said Rod. "There're only so many of these MRE packets left. We will need to make rescue happen sooner or later."

"Just like a Jesuit to eat all the food," said Ashton.

"How it was eaten was irrelevant," said Nata. "And I think that we can all take equal credit for the looming famine."

"What this really means," said Rod, "Is that either the person who put out the flares is shortsighted, but did not kill Ulysses, or else has a sinister plan, and did kill Ulysses."

"I tend to vote for the latter," said Jake.

"Any particular reason for that?" asked Guthrie. "Or just a revelation from on high?"

"A revelation from William of Ockham, actually," said Jake. *Do not multiply entities needlessly.*"

"It was probably really Duns Scotus who said that first," remarked Nata. "But of course, Ockham certainly said many very similar things. I belief Kaufmann makes that point."

"I'll kindly thank those of you who are not professional philosophers to stay in your own lanes," snapped Marcion.

"As your majesty decrees," murmured Ashton.

"Fear not," said Guthrie. "As a Christian pastor, our friend here is not allowed to use logic and reason. He must operate only by revelation and by faith."

"As G.K. Chesterton said in his short story, *The Blue Cross,* 'I know that people charge the Church with lowering reason, but it is just the other way. Alone on earth, the Church makes reason really supreme.' So reason is not really off the table just because I'm Christian," answered Jake.

"The church making reason supreme? Your church would collapse if your congregants truly thought things through," said Guthrie. "The quickest way to make an atheist is to have a Christian read the bible and to reason about it. Do you really think Jesus walked on water, and all that? It's simply impossible, and you know it."

"It's impossible by natural means," said Jake. "But no one says it happened by natural means. If Jesus had used some new and previously-unknown law of nature, then your refutation would have merit. But it's remarkable because it wasn't natural."

"So God-did-it," said Ashton. "That's the answer. I can't explain it, so God-did-it. Typical."

"Not what I said at all," said Jake. "And we're drifting far afield from our topic."

"Before we went down that rabbit hole, you were saying that you suspected one killer and one thief," said Rod, to Jake. "And not one person doing both."

"No, the opposite. It's unlikely for two people to be up to no good. It simplifies things if one person does it all. Only one killer; let's explore that – for now, let's assume that he had a good reason to kill Ulysses, and wasn't just a psychopath."

"He? You're ruling me out?" said Marcion.

"Yes, he just said that it definitely wasn't a psychopath," said Guthrie. Marcion glared at him.

"Let's assume that for now," said Jake. "And let's assume that all the rest of us would like to resume our normal lives as soon as possible."

"Granted, *ad argumentum*," said Nata.

"It follows, then, that the one person who may wish to keep us all here is the one who killed Ulysses. Either his intention is to kill all the rest of us, and thus prevent us from telling the police what happened, or it is to resolve some other small detail – find something hidden, find a secret that Ulysses held, or hide some bit of evidence."

"Evidence of what? What kind of evidence?" asked Nata, leaning forward in her seat.

"We can't know yet. Maybe that he is the killer, or maybe something else. But as an example of the type of thing that it could be: in Ulysses' garret, by his sleeping bag, there is a small pocket watch. Inside it is a photograph of two men. One appears to be a younger Ulysses. It is possible that if we knew the identity of the other man, we might know exactly why he was killed. So that watch might be the McGuffin – the bit of evidence that we're talking about."

"What did this other man look like?" asked Rod, with an amused grin. "Could he perhaps be one of us here tonight?"

"I doubt it," said Jake. "Unless I'm misjudging your ages, the other man would need to be in his seventies or eighties. Born around '52 or earlier. Give or take a couple years."

Guthrie raised his head and narrowed his eyes at Jake. "I was born in '49. What of it?"

"Nothing special, I suppose. But since we're on the topic, did you ever serve in the military, by any chance? Army, maybe, with a tour in South East Asia?"

"Ha! You're guessing! Most of the young men my age got drafted, so you assume we all were. That little Vietnam business. But I was too smart for that, by far. Spent most of that war up in Vancouver, B.C."

"In that case, it wouldn't be you in the photo."

"Not unless the alleged photo was taken in a small indy bookstore on Grenville Street. Or out in Stanley Park, by the trail through the woods. If there even is a photo."

"Then I can safely say that the man in the photo — a very real photo — is none of us, who are here now," said Jake. "But the other man might have been a father of one of us, or an uncle, or an older cousin, or some other kind of relation. My great-uncle, perhaps."

"Grasping for straws," said Ashton.

"The connection seems tenuous," said Jake. "But that's just an example of the sort of thing that a person might be searching for — and the sort of thing that would make him want to keep us all here until he found it."

"Bring down this alleged watch," suggested Ashton. "See who steals it. Then we'll have our killer."

"The watch was just a hypothetical example," said Jake. "It might have nothing to do with the killer at all."

"So you lied to us," said Marcion.

"Just like a — Oof!" said Ashton, as Guthrie jabbed him with an elbow.

"No lie. There is a watch," said Jake. "And there's a photo. But it may bear no significance. Or it might be the critical key to the entire thing."

"Why should we believe you?" asked Marcion.

"You shouldn't," said Jake, as he got up to see if there were any spaghetti left. Sadly, the noodles were mostly gone, although there was a small supply of the excellent sauce. He suspected that Nata and Rod had supplemented the sauce with ketchup and flavoring packets, leftover from some of the previous MRE meals.

Despite its tasty flavor, Marcion had declared it the worst spaghetti sauce in the history of tomatoes, and Ashton had lamented that they were mere miles from the fine dining restaurants over on the peninsula. Jake didn't see anything wrong with it at all, and put a healthy extra dollop atop the few remaining noodles.

He wondered what Bryly was having for dinner, and wished he were there, with her. The food may or may not have been better, but the company would have been vastly superior. But then, he supposed, he might have been biased.

As he made his way back into the parlor, Ashton laid aside his own plate and turned to Jake.

"So, you seem to be a fan of Lewis," he said.

"I am a great fan," said Jake. "I can't wait to meet him." He twirled his fork in the noodles, wrapping them around the tines in a whirlwind of pasta.

"Good luck with that," said Marcion. "He's dead."

"Yes, but that's not incurable," said Jake.

"So, if you're such a Lewis fan, what do you think of his famous trilemma?" asked Ashton.

"Trilemma? You mean the poached egg?"

"Poached egg?"

"Yes. It's the argument from Mere Christianity, concerning Christ not being merely an ordinary man. It's often called Lewis' trilemma, but it was Josh McDowell who later formalized Lewis' argument as a trilemma. What Lewis said was that we shouldn't go around calling Jesus a good teacher. If he was not in fact God, then he was either a cruel liar, or else a lunatic like a man who thinks he's a poached egg."

"But that Lord, Liar, Lunatic business?"

"As a protest against sloppy thinking? That's Lewis. As an abductive argument? That's McDowell."

94

"Okay, anyway, what do you think of it?"

"It's a solid argument. A limited set of possibilities exist. Eliminate the wrong ones, and you're left with the right one."

"False trilemma," said Marcion.

"Why a false trilemma?" said Jake.

"Because I know any argument where a Christian presents limited options is always a false dilemma or false trilemma. They try to narrow the choices down to two, and then steer you into their answer. Accept the premise, accept the bit."

Jake took a last bite of noodle, sopped the last sauce with a bread-like substance from an MRE, and smiled. "If the trilemma is false, what's the other choice? What possibility should we be considering?"

"Legend," said Guthrie. "Maybe he never existed."

Jake sipped water and leaned back in his chair. "Alright, well, if we're going to cover every possibility, then we need to start at the root. Either Jesus was a historical person or he was not. If not, then He was a legend.

"But he's mentioned by many secular historians. Tacitus, Suetonius, Dio Cassius, Lucian of Samosata … That's just to name a few, off the top of my head. In all, from all sources, forty or more writers mention him, including nine or ten who were secular or pagan, and thus were speaking against interest.

"He certainly existed historically. So either he was merely a good teacher, or he was a teacher who said that He was God incarnate. If the former is true, then He was a lama."

"He was a llama?" asked Ashton. "Now I'm envisioning an alpaca preaching. 'Repennnnnnt.' Ha!"

"No, I mean the one-L kind of a lama. A guru, a religious teacher, or a moralist."

"Reminds me of that Ogden Nash poem," said Nata. "But you're on a roll, so don't let me interrupt."

"So was He just a moral teacher? Well, everything we have that indicates the nature of His teaching – every example is saturated with claims of deity. And we see that reflected in the reactions of the listeners – all the times that they tried to throw

Him off a cliff, or took up rocks to stone Him, or tore their clothes – those are reactions to what they saw as blasphemy."

"He never once said He was God," said Guthrie.

"Matthew 26, verse 63. The high priest forced Him to speak by invoking God. To refuse to answer would itself be blasphemy. The only safe answer would be for Him to say, 'No, I'm not God.' The oath demanded an explicit affirmation or an explicit denial.

"But instead, Jesus says, in the next verse, 'It is as you have said,' and then He says that they will see Him descending from the clouds in glory. And they took that as a claim of deity – which it obviously was – and they tore their clothes."

"What has tearing clothes to do with anything?" snapped Marcion. "So they got mad. So what?"

"It's the prescribed reaction for blasphemy, spoken in the presence of a rabbi. He must tear his clothes and put dirt or ashes on his head. When we see that reaction, it indicates that what was just said seems blasphemous."

"So you have one verse in your book, so it must be true. Typical," said Ashton. "Building an entire doctrine on a verse."

"It is truly a valid criticism that we have no claims of His deity outside your book," said Rod. "You're kind of using your book to prove your book."

"To answer Ashton first," said Jake, "There are many claims of deity by Jesus in the gospels. In addition to things he said, such as John 8:58, or John 4:26, He also accepted worship, healed the sick, and forgave sins. Those are actions reserved for God." He drank from his water, but the flavor of the sauce remained. Given a choice, he'd have had a bit more of the spaghetti. A faint trace of the flavor remained in his mouth, calling for a further taste.

"Rod, on your point, we're talking about what Jesus taught, and the best source for that would logically be His own disciples. But there are distinct claims that support Jesus' deity, or that he claimed it, from outside the bible, and some of them are by hostile witnesses. For example, when Celsus claims that

Jesus did His miracles by sorcery, he's tacitly admitting that Jesus did actual miracles. Or when Josephus says that Jesus did startling works; we can't be certain what he meant, but it sounds like a convincing sign of some sort."

"Or that most people commonly believed that he did them," said Rod. "Historians would report what was said of people, and not necessarily what was true about them."

"Fair enough," said Jake, "But where would they have gotten that idea? Obviously, from the apostles. The embedded creed in 1st Corinthians, the one taught to Paul by Peter and James – That creed was composed within weeks, or at the very outside within months, of the crucifixion. Paul confirms in his letter to the Galatians that he compared his teachings to those of Peter and James at least twice; once while John was also there with them. So they were all teaching Jesus' deity."

"They got it wrong. They misunderstood," said Rod. "Suppose that Jesus never said a thing about deity, and the disciples just assumed it." He nodded to Jake's water glass. "Would you like some wine? We have a good cellar, at least."

"I'm fine with this," he said. "But here's the problem: If a teacher has twelve disciples, and every single one of them misunderstands his message so badly that they think he was claiming to be God, even though he clearly wasn't – Well, can we call such a man a good teacher? Or even a moralist?"

"The deity claims came later," said Guthrie. "Over the course of the three hundred years until the Bible was codified. After all the principals were long dead and gone." He sipped his whiskey. "Your first complete Bible dates to, what, 350 or so?"

"That doesn't work for a couple of reasons," said Jake. "First, that embedded creed we mentioned. Second, we have Pliny the younger, right around the turn of the first century, telling the emperor Trajan that these Christians sing a hymn to Jesus, as to a god." Jake shrugged. "That's only about twenty or so years after John's gospel was written.

"And to top it off, we have the P52 fragment. It's a small bit of papyrus, a few verses from John 18, and it dates to around 150 AD, give or take. Polycarp, John's disciple, died around 155, so this might have been from a copy of John made during his lifetime. And the verses on it are the passage where Jesus admits his Deity to Pilate. So this is not some late teaching. The earliest Christians clearly believed Jesus truly was God incarnate."

"That does close the door on Him being a lama," said Nata. "And it's a relief not to have a picture of a holy alpaca in my mind. But there's still the other – "

"Not so fast," said Guthrie. "That they believed He was God still doesn't make Him God."

"No," said Jake, "But it supports that He claimed to be God. At this point, we're just closing the door on Him being a lama. G.K. Chesterton put it like this: The fact that people thought He was claiming deity is as unique as the claim itself. No one ever got the idea that Mohammad was claiming to be God, or that Buddha made such a claim, or Confucius, or Lao Tze. Not one Jew in the history of the world has ever confused Moses, or even Abraham, with their God.

"But the followers of Jesus all, universally, without exception, believed that He claimed to be God. For them to believe that idea falsely would be more remarkable, and less probable, than for Jesus to actually be God incarnate. So the fact that we, here, are having this very conversation, right now, strongly suggests that He did, indeed, make that claim."

At that exact moment, the lights went out.

"I suppose you think that your God has spoken," snarled Marcion. "A divine proof of some kind."

"Not at all," said Jake.

"More likely the electric bill is among those not paid recently," said Rod. "Does anyone happen to know?"

"We might be a little bit overdue," said Guthrie. "Now that you mention it, I seem to recall an invoice."

"I don't suppose we have candles?" said Nata.

"Are you really afraid of the dark?" asked Marcion. "Don't worry, your pet preacher will keep you safe."

"Safety is actually the issue," said Rod. "If we sleep like we did last night, those on watch will have trouble making sure the killer isn't plying his trade."

"The descent of darkness is a sign of the ignorance of the people in this room," pronounced Guthrie. "The preacher has spoken so much nonsense that he has robbed us of all light. It is a metaphor for the ignorance flooding the room."

"No, it's real," said Nata.

"Socrates would say that this would be a truly great talent to have," said Rod. "For the one who has power to corrupt someone's reason surely also has power to improve him, and in similar measure. One with the power to create darkness in your mind would have the power, as well, to enlighten."

"Socrates was an idiot," said Marcion.

A light flicked on; a single point of light, hovering above Nata's lap. In the complete dark, it seemed like a search beam. Jake put his hand between the light and his eyes.

"Sorry," said Nata. "I've just remembered that I have this." She saw them covering their eyes, and pointed the light away from them, lighting up a corner of the room. Shadows seemed to dance as she waved the tiny flashlight.

"Our watchers will have at least one tool," said Rod. "Well done, Nata."

It was a few minutes after eight when there was a knock at Bryly's door. She had been sitting, staring at the pages of a murder mystery for the last hour. She couldn't say that she'd really been reading, because her thoughts were not on the book at all. She was too busy worrying about Jake. In fact, she could not have described the book at all, were she asked.

She laid down the book and peeked through the peephole, then opened the door wide to the two ladies on the step.

"Thao Trang, Reyna, what brings you out so late?"

"We were concerned about you," said Reyna. "We want to make sure you're okay, with Jake being away."

"Well, thank you. Would you like to come in?"

Of course, the living room, which a moment ago had seemed fine to her, immediately seemed to be an unredeemable mess. She bent to pick up a couch pillow that had fallen into the floor, but couldn't reach it.

Reyna grabbed the pillow and tossed it onto the couch before taking Bryly's elbow.

"Don't worry about that," said Reyna. "We're not here to check on your housekeeping."

"Is there any news of Jake?" asked Thao Trang, as Reyna guided Bryly to a chair.

"Nothing yet," said Bryly, as she sank down into the overstuffed armchair. "I did file a missing person report with the Emeryville police. They were able to confirm that he got off the train there. He joined with three other people, and they all got into a small bus – kind of like a tour bus, or those really short transit busses."

"Were they able to trace the movements of the bus?"

"No, there are too many private bus companies in the bay area. I let them know that it was supposed to be some sort of an island estate."

"Hard to reach an island by bus," said Reyna.

"Well, we don't know if they really meant a true island," said Thao Trang. "Sometimes peninsulas are called islands. Long Island, for example."

"I believe that Father Somers said it was an actual island, but to be honest, I wasn't paying attention," said Bryly.

"There are not many in the bay. I think they are not on Alcatraz. Chi Due, his boat is from Moss Landing. I told him: tomorrow he will go up to the bay, to look for islands."

"That's very kind," said Bryly. "But I can't ask that…"

"Pastor Jake was with us when everyone thought my husband killed that crazy man, that Amos."

"And it's our duty as the wives of deacons," said Reyna, "to uphold the wife of the pastor. And we're your friends."

"Well, I'm glad you're here. The police said they'd send a helicopter tomorrow, to scan the islands out in the bay – there aren't very many of them, apparently. I mean, really, Alcatraz is the only one I can think of offhand, and as you said, that's not too likely for a retreat."

"I'm sure he'll be fine," said Reyna. "It's just a matter of time. Can I put on some tea? Would that be alright?"

"It would be nice," said Bryly.

"Also," said Thao Trang, "We want to talk about the outreach for Saturday, next week. We have lots of fliers ready."

Jake sat in the dark, letting silence hide him. The room had gotten very quiet. The only light was from Nata's flashlight, which she had placed into a water glass. The beam pointed to the ceiling, giving a dim light to the entire room.

When the clock struck eight, Nata and Marcion had volunteered to take the first watch. Marcion had said that it was the only way she'd get decent sleep without some idiot waking her for her turn. Guthrie had made a remark under his breath to Ashton, who had chuckled, but there the matter had stopped.

Jake slipped his shoes off and waited a moment longer, listening to the room. Faint snores were audible, and no one was looking his way. He quietly fluffed up his bedding and placed a couch pillow under it to simulate his chest, then he slid out from under the makeshift coverings.

Again, he paused. In the faint light, he could just make out that the three other men each had their eyes closed. Marcion was facing away from him, and Nata was quietly staring at a large painting over the mantel.

Jake crouched beside his chair. If he moved slowly, in tiny stages, he thought he could make it into the drawing room without crossing Nata or Marcion's field of vision. His ears strained at the near-silence.

With a shoe in each hand, he slowly duck-walked sideways, staying in the shadow of his chair. So long as the shadow was between him and the light, he should be out of view of the watchers. He ducked behind an immense vase and paused again.

No sound betrayed alarm. The men emitted soft snores. He peeked one eye around the vase. Marcion was still facing away from him and Nata seemed to be looking at the painting.

He stood. Distance and darkness made him feel more secure. He took two gliding steps towards the drawing room door, and paused just over the threshold, where the room was absolutely pitch black.

From the inky night, he moved one eye back into the parlor for one last glance at his sleeping comrades. Nata's face was turned towards him, and she seemed to be staring right at him. He froze.

Her pupils were shrouded by her brow, so he couldn't tell what she saw, if anything. She might just be looking at the shadows on the wall, or staring into space and daydreaming. It was impossible to tell at that distance.

He willed his chest to rise and fall as slowly as possible. Even so, it seemed like she must hear the beating of his heart. After a second, she slowly turned her face back to the painting on the wall.

Jake pulled his own face back into the drawing room, and quietly made his way through the dim room. He moved slowly in the blackness, feeling his way with his hands, pausing to dodge furniture, decorations, and other obstacles. When he had made his way safely out of the room, he sat down on the floor to put on his shoes.

With his shoes on, he would make even more noise, so he carefully lifted his foot only millimeters for each step, pausing a second before lifting the other foot. It seemed to take hours to reach the hallway carpet.

It was perhaps an hour and a half, or maybe two hours later, when he slipped back into the room again. The flashlight was out. He couldn't say if it were because the batteries had gone dead, or if Nata had turned it off to save them. The latter case was the most dangerous. If Nata and Marcion were sitting in this profound darkness, by now their eyesight would be at its most sensitive.

He crept haltingly across the floor in his sock feet, pausing often to listen. He turned his head in all directions, but there was not even the faintest glimmer of light. The room was silent as a library during spring break.

When his fingers finally brushed his chair – hopefully it was his and not Guthrie's – he put down his shoes, laying one on its side as if he had kicked them off to sleep. With gentle hands, he lifted the bedding, and carefully checked that the chair was vacant.

Only the pillow was there; the one that he had left in place of his torso. In slow and careful stages, he slid under the covers. He tried to put the pillow under his head, but it seemed snagged on something, so he left it where it was and rested his head on the upholstery.

Two hours, give or take, until his watch. He closed his eyes to nap until they awakened him. Broken sleep: two hours now, a watch, and then however long from then until daylight, would leave him groggy in the morning. But it couldn't be helped. In moments, his snores joined the others.

Bryly made her way up the stairs. Her first thought, when she saw the women at the door, had been to be a bit insulted. They thought that just because Jake was gone for a couple nights, she needed her hand held?

And then she had realized that their company felt really good. It wasn't their expressions of reassurance, or even their concern for her in general, so much as how it normalized things. Having them there made it seem so ordinary, and not at all like the sort of night where bad news crouches at the door.

For the first time in two days, Bryly smiled. She would need to do something nice for the ladies, to show her appreciation. She slid into bed, still smiling, and thanked God for her friends before falling fast asleep.

Chapter Eleven

JAKE AWOKE WITH LIGHT streaming into the room. He was disoriented for a moment. He looked around. Guthrie, Ashton, Rod, and Marcion were snoring in harmony. Nata was not in the chair where he had seen her last.

He snapped awake and leapt to his feet.

Nata was sprawled on the floor.

"A little help here!" he shouted, as he knelt beside her.

Rod gave a snort.

Guthrie growled. "What's all the ruckus?"

"Nata. She's been hurt!" Jake felt for her pulse and found it. He could see her chest move, so he knew she was breathing. There was a small bloody spot on the back of her head.

"Did she fall and hit her head on something?" asked Rod.

"I doubt it," said Jake, as he shook her shoulder. "Things have just gotten more serious."

"I'll say," said Ashton, pointing to Jake's chair. A large kitchen knife was sticking out of his bedding, handle towards them. "Someone tried to kill you in your sleep."

Nata rolled onto her side and sat up. "Where am I?" she asked. "What happened?"

"We should ask you," said Ashton. "You were supposed to be keeping watch."

"We bravely and sacrificially refrained from waking any of you," said Marcion, "And this is the thanks we get. Knocked out cold, and then maligned for having been unconscious, against our wills, for a mere fraction of the night."

"In other words, you were asleep and missed everything," said Guthrie.

"Being struck on the head leaves one little choice."

"I see blood on Nata's head, but not on yours," said Rod.

"For all we know, she's the one who struck Nata," said Ashton. "Waited until she looked away and POW!"

"She does hate Jake," said Guthrie.

"She hates everyone," said Ashton. "It's all part of her schtick. The grumpy old woman archetype."

"Do you suppose that we should check the knife for fingerprints?" asked Ashton.

"How would we do that?" snarled Marcion. "We have no means to take fingerprints, nor to compare them."

"And the attacker would have wiped the handle, without any doubt," said Rod.

"So why didn't Jake die?" asked Guthrie.

"He's really good at not doing that," said Nata. "But we're getting off topic." She started to stand up, and winced.

"I really hope that it's not any of us," said Ashton. "The idea that someone could be standing here, calmly discussing head trauma as if we were talking about the weather, and really be a cold-blooded killer – It chills my blood."

"Speaking of chilly blood," said Rod, "I'll go and put on some coffee. Nata will surely need a warm beverage after her ordeal last night."

"Isn't the power out?" said Guthrie.

"The oven is wood-fired," said Rod.

"What will they think of next?" asked Ashton.

"While he's out of the room, I move that we reject Rod's membership in the Organization," said Marcion. "He's been spending far too much time agreeing with the preacher. Let's recall him and throw him out on his ear."

"That's exactly the sort of thing we're against," said Nata. "We're free-thinkers, and that means that we must be able to think freely – to go against the flow of the zeitgeist, to hold our own opinions despite the disagreement of our peers."

"We only say that when the majority is Christian," said Ashton. "Do you think we'd just let, say, a Christian into the Organization, just because he said he had reached his views as a result of logic and careful thought?"

"There's Father Spike," said Nata. "He was even one of the founders, after all." She touched the top of her head and winced, sucking a breath through her teeth.

"Spike was about as Christian as Ramadan," said Guthrie. "He only wore a collar because he felt it gave him *gravitas*."

"And he wasn't overly concerned with *veritas*," said Ashton.

"He felt that an attack on Christianity felt like it carried more weight when it came from a minister of that faith. After all, those Christians are just little sheep, following their pastor from pasture to pasture." Guthrie looked towards the dining room door. "Where's that coffee?" he asked.

"I'm kind of shocked. I get knocked unconscious, Jake gets almost stabbed, and you're concerned about whether you can kick someone out for fraternizing with the enemy?" asked Nata.

"You're one to talk about fraternization," said Marcion.

"How do we know that you were really knocked out?" asked Guthrie. "You could have just shirked your duties, laid down on the floor, and gone to sleep."

"After knocking me out," said Marcion, with an indignant tone. "Betraying your own watch ... co-watcher ... whatever it's called. Your peer. Your compatriot."

"You were snoring the second you sat down," said Nata. "And that's why there's not a knot on top of your head."

"You should have that looked at," said Ashton. "Too bad we haven't got any servants about."

"Forget that for a moment," she said. "Don't any of you realize that any one of us might have been killed last night?"

"Because of you shirking your duties," said Guthrie. "You really let us all down."

"How do we know Marcion didn't do it?" asked Ashton. "It accounts for all we know. She might have smacked Nata upside the head – and let's face it, we've all wanted to do that. Then she could easily stick the knife into Jake, who, fortunately, happened to be a pillow."

"Nice of you to think it fortunate," said Jake.

"Fortunate for you," said Ashton. "I'm not sure it matters to the rest of us. I mean, it would surely have been tragic. And very traumatic. We'd have to see all that blood."

"He's right about one thing, at least," said Jake, to Nata. "We should look at that lump. Let's go in the kitchen and clean that wound a bit."

"While you're in there, find out what's keeping the coffee," shouted Guthrie, to their retreating backs.

The kitchen had fewer windows than the parlor, and was thus slightly gloomy in the early morning light. Rod was feeding thin sticks of wood into a recalcitrant oven, trying in vain to channel a stream of flame and hot air up to the cooktop, where a lonely percolator sat waiting.

"Never realized how long it takes one of these things to get going," he said. "Victorians must have spent all of their time feeding their fires."

"A lot of cold steel to warm up," said Jake. "I guess it's understandable that it's slow." He turned a wooden ladder-back chair so that its back was to the window. Nata sat down on it, facing the stove.

"You're looking rather sanguine about last night's murder attempt," said Rod. "If it had been me, I think I'd be a bit more upset than you appear. Orders of magnitude."

"It seems a bit surreal," said Jake, as he dampened a tea towel and pressed it to the wound on Nata's head. "I think it just hasn't hit me yet. I doubt if I'll sleep at all tonight."

The percolator gurgled, and gave a single anemic perk. After a moment, it repeated, then perked three times in a row.

"Well, progress at last," said Nata, watching the clear liquid in the sight glass. "Coffee to the rescue."

"It'll take a while to brew," said Rod. "So, Jake, any more thoughts on who might have done it? The pillow-stabbing, I mean, and, of course, the assault on Nata."

"From a standpoint of opportunity, it's wide open," said Jake. "I can eliminate myself. And I have trouble believing that Nata would do it, or that she could have done this to herself."

"A little bit off-handed, as exonerations go, but I'll take it," said Nata. "Ouch."

"Sorry, I'll try to be gentler."

"On the other hand, it was very nice to have a full night's sleep," said Rod.

"You're not exactly welcome," said Nata.

"I'm not a professional," said Jake, "But it looks like you won't need stitches. Still, one of us should stay with you for the rest of the day. If you feel light-headed, dizzy, get a severe headache, one of your eyes goes out of focus…"

"Out of focus? What would cause that?"

"Well, again, I'm not a professional. But one of the symptoms of certain kinds of brain injury, they say, is that one pupil suddenly dilates. And that would change the depth of field, like a wide-open f-stop on an old camera."

"Ah," she said. "And so the background would go blurry."

"So I assume," said Jake. "But I'm not a professional."

"Moral of the story, someone needs to be with you at all times," said Rod. "I nominate Jake … Hello, what's this?"

Rod bent forward and tugged a scrap of paper from under the edge of the oven. It was from a yellow pad, of the sort used by lawyers, and one edge was torn. The other three edges were burned. There was writing, in block letters.

"Someone was using the oven as an incinerator," said Nata. "What does it say?"

"Can't tell who wrote it, with the letters squared off like this," said Rod, "But it appears to say, 'Cion,' then a line break, 'him dead,' line break, a string of numbers, and then 'ysses.' I presume that last bit should be, 'Ulysses,' but I can't be sure."

He proffered the scrap to Nata, who stared at it without reaching for it. Jake opened a cabinet beside the sink and pulled out a small zipper bag. As he held it towards Rod, Rod dropped the scrap inside it.

"Well, an interesting twist," said Rod. "Possibly a clue to motive, or at least to premeditation."

"Block letters suggest a deliberate attempt at anonymity," said Nata. "And I suppose that 'cion' could be the last part of Marcion. You see where the burned edge crosses by the c."

"It could also be a word like suspicion," said Jake. "I found some rubbing alcohol. If you're okay with that, I'll just pat some on the wound."

"I suppose it's better than peroxide."

"It's going to sting a bit, but at least you won't turn into a platinum blonde." He touched the cloth gently to her head, patting the edges of the wound. "Hopefully that will stave off infection until your doctor can see you."

"Should we put Marcion down for the crime?" asked Rod.

"I'm still not ready to commit to a theory of the crime," said Jake. "So we can't go jumping to a conclusion."

"I got the idea, from things you've said, that you've worked with the police before," said Nata.

"Not exactly. You know the euphemism that they use on TV, about 'Helping the police with their inquiries?' Well, most of my interactions with police have been like that. Though there is a detective who attends the church."

"You've been arrested?" asked Rod, with a grin. "That is the last thing I expected."

"Questioned," said Jake. "At various times, Bryly and I have been suspected of things like shooting at the governor, stabbing a parishioner, and eating poisoned fish. But of course, we didn't do any of those things."

"Interesting resumé for a pastor." Rod returned to staring at the scrap. "Perhaps we were slightly hasty in assuming your innocence." A smirk betrayed him. "We might want to offer you membership after all."

"I've done all I can do here," said Jake, to Nata. "The bleeding has stopped, there doesn't appear to be any other damage, and as long as you don't decide to take a nap, I think it's probably going to be okay."

"Like you, I doubt I'll sleep tonight," said Nata. "Thanks for checking it out, though. I feel a little bit better about it." She stood up and pushed the chair back under the adjacent table.

The coffee was perking steadily now. The color of the fluid was beginning to change to a very pale brown. Rod nodded to the sight glass atop the percolator lid.

"I'll wait for this to finish brewing," said Rod.

"We'll see you in the other room," said Nata.

Guthrie viewed them with suspicion as they came back into the parlor. "You were gone a long time," he said. "Plotting to kill us all in our sleep?"

"No, I don't believe that came up at all," said Nata.

"But the coffee should be ready in about ten minutes or so. It's perking nicely," said Jake.

"Percolators," muttered Marcion. "The very worst way to make coffee. Guaranteed to ruin the flavor. It's like a slap in the face. A veritable slap in the face."

"And the only one available at the moment," said Nata. "So did you manage to purge the Organization's rolls, while we were all away?"

"No," said Ashton. "Unfortunately, we'll need your dues to keep the lights on."

"Once we get them back on," said Guthrie.

Rod chose that moment to emerge from the kitchen, with the percolator and a stack of mugs on a silver salver. He had even managed to find a small sleeve of shortbread cookies.

"The breakfast is served, such as it is," he said.

"It certainly puts the *petit* in *petit dejeuner*," said Marcion.

"Think of it as a continental breakfast," said Nata.

110

"I had a thought," said Rod, as he poured himself a cup, added a splash of cream and a spoon of sugar, then tasted it. "There were eight chicken dishes."

"Yes, we know," said Marcion. "And that sorry excuse for a gluttonous preacher ate two of them."

"We can't know who ate the eighth pie," said Nata. "At least, not at the moment. You were saying, Rod?"

"Why were eight prepared? Why not only seven?"

"It's a round number," said Guthrie.

"Perhaps the cook was intending to eat one," said Ashton. "Why does it matter?"

"It matters because it implies that there should have been eight of us for dinner, instead of merely seven," said Jake. "A nice point, Rod. It hadn't occurred to me."

"If the cook were making food for the servants, they'd all have had one baking. There would have been nine or ten, instead of eight," said Nata.

"Maybe they only had eight pans, and they were going to make more once we were served," said Marcion.

"Anything is possible," said Rod. "But I think we should carefully consider what it means if there were to have been eight attendees for dinner."

"Perhaps the killer had another victim, before Ulysses?" asked Nata. "Is that what you're getting at?"

"Or perhaps Mr. Eight – Or Ms. Eight – is the real killer." Rod picked up a shortbread cookie and touched it briefly to his coffee before popping it into his mouth.

"So you propose," said Guthrie, "That there's someone else, a stranger to us all, hiding somewhere here in the building? And that he killed Ulysses?"

"The servants would have had the guest list," said Nata. "So only they would know who to expect. We were, for the most part, strangers to each other. Until the other night."

"Are we multiplying entities?" asked Ashton. "We don't even know that this Octavius even exists. There's no evidence, not one shred."

"There's the eighth chicken pie," said Rod. "That must mean something." He shrugged, and managed not to spill his coffee while doing it.

"And the theory has explanatory power," said Nata.

"Certainly food for thought," said Jake. "But if this eighth person exists, what tells us that he is the killer?"

"He has chosen to hide from us," said Guthrie. "Assuming he exists, he'd have no reason to play hide and seek."

"Unless he's a victim," said Nata. "Since we didn't know he was here, we wouldn't have known to look for him. Or perhaps he has a good reason, unknown to us. Maybe he saw the killer murder Ulysses."

"You're all just getting Stockholm syndrome," snapped Marcion. "You've been stuck together for two days, and now you're feeling affectionate. Aww, that's so cute. So you're willing to invent an eighth person out of thin air, and that way none of these folks, whom you now love, have to be the killer."

The sarcasm hung in the air for a moment.

"Well," said Jake, "I do hate the idea that any of you tried to stab me in my sleep, but I'm still willing to face the fact that one of you very likely did."

"You did that yourself," said Marcion. "You just love the attention, and you don't have a congregation readily at hand to fawn over you. You slid that knife right through the blanket, pushed a pillow onto it, and then acted surprised when you awakened. Admit it."

"I deny doing it, for what that's worth," said Jake.

"Of course you'd say that," said Marcion.

"Rod, what did you do to put this smokey flavor into the coffee?" asked Nata.

"Nothing special," he said. "And I hadn't noticed the smokey flavor until now. Rather nice, like a trace of that tea, that Lapsang Soochong. Except that it's coffee."

"If the gourmets can contain themselves," said Guthrie, "Would someone please explain where this eighth person was supposed to sleep?"

112

"Good point," said Ashton, in a begrudging tone. "There are three rooms on each floor, all occupied."

"And Ulysses slept in the garret, above my room," said Guthrie. "So unless this eighth person was planning to sleep on the drawing room sofa, there aren't enough rooms."

"Maybe he killed Ulysses for his bed," said Ashton.

"That would be a monumentally bad choice," said Rod. "Since Ulysses had only a sleeping bag on a hard floor."

"But did the eighth person know that?" asked Ashton. "Or he might have mistaken him for someone else."

"Maybe he didn't plan to sleep at all, but merely to kill us in our beds," said Nata. "He may hate us equally. In which case, we all owe Jake our lives."

"Also, he cured cancer, arranged world peace, and took out the trash without being asked," said Marcion. "Give it a break."

"An eighth pie is not sufficient reason to assume an eighth guest," said Guthrie. "That's the point I'm trying to make."

"Let's hold it in abeyance for now," said Rod. "Pending other evidence that we may turn up later."

"Maybe there's a legion of angels dancing on the heads of pins," snarled Marcion. "Maybe this pastor let them in."

"Canonically," said Jake, "If an angel wants a person dead, he doesn't use a pepper grinder or a knife."

"Maybe these particular angels like to play fair with their victims," said Marcion. "Oh, never mind."

"Weren't you supposed to bring a wife?" asked Rod. "As I recall, the invitation was for Mr. and Mrs." He chuckled. "At the time, I remember thinking it very odd for a priest to actually have a wife."

"I am told," said Jake, "That if an Anglican priest who is married converts to the RCC, he is not required to divorce his wife. I believe it's considered water under the bridge."

"You're not Anglican," snapped Marcion.

"No, but we Baptists are also allowed to marry. As to why she's not here: She's quite pregnant, and we both thought it best for her to stay home."

"Poor oppressed woman," said Marcion.

Ashton sipped his coffee. "That is a strong smokey flavor," he said. "It's a bit like Turkish coffee blended with a Scottish breakfast tea."

"That would taste horrid," said Nata.

"Yes, coffee and tea don't mix," said Guthrie.

"There's no smoke flavor in the coffee," said Jake.

"You're crazy," said Ashton. "Don't you taste that?"

"It's not from the coffee," said Jake. "Look." He pointed through the parlor, and out the french doors, into the hillside beyond, where a steady stream of smoke could be seen rising into the sky.

"Oh dear," said Nata. "That's not good. Does that mean what I think it means?"

"Yes," said Jake. "If what you think it means is that the island is on fire."

Chapter Twelve

THERE WERE, INDEED, FLAMES.

The turf, which had been mostly dry until the recent rains, was smoldering down the island from the northern point of the island, nearest the bridge. From time to time, a particularly dry patch of wild oats or bearded darnel would flare up. A charred sagebrush on the northern slope was barely visible over the low ridge, and the smell of burnt sage hung heavily in the air.

The heat of the advancing fire dried the grass ahead of it, sending steam to blend with the smoke, and gradually speeding the spread of the flames. Clouds of steam and smoke rose above the island, high into the sky, like a thunderhead, though white and stained with streaks of yellowish brown. Tall yellow flames framed in smoke danced along the burning front.

A short ridge extended away from them to the northeast, narrowing quickly to a knife edge. One finger of the fire, driven by the wind, raced along that ridge, engulfing a small scrub oak tree. They watched as the tree went up like a torch, suddenly aflame. The burning leaves and twigs fell beneath the low spreading branches, forming a bed of embers that would slowly doom even the most resistant of bark layers.

It was like something out of a movie, and in some ways it seemed to be in slow motion. And yet, even as they stared, the blaze also marched steadily towards the house. The rippling heat waves may it difficult to gauge the distance to the fire line. It looked as if it were far away, and at once very near; in any case a present and an imminent danger.

"What do we do?" shouted Guthrie. "It'll burn down the house!" He looked desperately towards Rod, and then towards Jake, as if expecting a plan. Rod shrugged.

"Have we got any shovels?" asked Jake. "I think I saw a tool shed over there, towards the ridge."

Rod jogged in the direction Jake had pointed, and came back with an awkward armload of gardening tools, from rakes and shovels to hoes and hatchets. Jake grabbed one and pushed a square shovel into Guthrie's hands.

"Start near the house, maybe ten feet upwind, and try to scrape about three feet wide of clear soil. We need a firebreak."

"Shouldn't it be wider?"

"We're lucky: the wind is wrong, and the grass is still very wet. In these conditions, I don't think it will be able to jump a three-foot gap. And we don't have time to make it wider."

Nata grabbed another shovel. "I'll help him," she said, as she started scratching at the grass.

"I can't do that," said Ashton. "My heart won't take it."

"Find a hose," said Jake. "Wetting the grass on each side of the firebreak will increase its effectiveness."

"In the movies, they do backfires," said Rod.

"If we had something reliable to light fires with, it might be effective," said Jake.

Rod pointed to a cardboard box, with a small blue tarp neatly folded on top of it. The side of the box was marked with the word "Fusees."

"Where did that come from?" asked Jake.

"Cincinnati, originally," said Rod. "But for now, it looks like they came out of hiding."

"Let's take a couple of them and try to burn out a dead zone," said Jake. "We'll start farther from the house, and try to give the firebreak crew a little more time."

Jake and Rod took up positions between the fire and the house. Jake struck a flare and held it to the grass. The grass was reluctant, but started to smolder after a moment. He took three paces to his right and did it again. He started four or five spots before looking back.

The first spot had expanded into an egg shape, small end towards the fire, about four feet around at the big end. It was growing fastest on the side towards him, and a close second on the side towards the house. Jake ran back to the first circle and started to stamp down the growing flames, carefully keeping one foot in the black. His feet felt hot, through his shoes, but he decided that it was only in his mind.

With the grass burning sluggishly from the dampness, he was able to stomp out the burning edge of the fire along the side that faced the house, but the approaching blaze loomed ever nearer. By the time he reached the second growing circle, the near edge of that circle was almost to the black sooty zone of the first one. He let it burn to him, bridging the gap, before he started treading the near edge of the second circle. Cinders and fine black dust rose from each step as he trod it down.

The flare burned down too close to his hand, so he threw it into the soot zone and pulled another from his back pocket. The stub rolled into a patch of unburned grass, and briefly flared up as flames.

Far to his left, Ashton had found a slender green garden hose, and a faucet. A bronze spray nozzle, at the tip of the hose, made a tight conical spread of water. The navy would have called it a low-pressure fog, and there would have been a second hose alongside with a high-pressure stream, to rip apart combustibles, soaking them into submission.

Jake wished, in that moment, for a three-inch navy fire hose, with its high-pressure stream drawing from a fully-pressurized fire main. It would have made short work of the approaching fire line, soaking the ground into mud as it tore the grass from the earth.

Instead, there was only Ashton's one lazy cone of water, streaming a few feet ahead of Ashton, and the gentle wind spray, blowing off of it as a fine overhead mist. The mist drifted on the wind, often landing in the burned zone Jake had created.

Ashton looked like a suburban grandfather out watering his lawn. Sunlight sparkled through the mist, making tiny shimmering rainbows. All he needed was a pair of sandals, with white socks.

Behind Ashton, a small distance back, Marcion pointed and gestured, staring at Ashton. Her words didn't quite bridge the distance all the way to Jake, but he heard the tone and the form of the words. He was pretty sure he didn't need to know anything more.

Jake finished trampling out the third and fourth backfires before striking the fresh flare that was in his hand. Rod, off to Jake's right, had made a long black streak with his first flare, from the edge of the eastward cut and inward about sixty yards, but it was farther upwind than Jake's. Rod was presently off by the cliff, stomping out the last stretch of the near edge.

The grassfire was speeding up now, and the flames were leaping higher. Either the grass was drier now, or else the fire was quickly drying the fuel ahead of it. There was still a huge gap between Jake and Rod. Jake struggled to gauge how quickly the flame front would reach the gap.

A tiny sagebrush to Jake's left was engulfed by the front, and went up like a torch, throwing flaming leaves on the wind and making a bulge in the fire line. The branches crackled and hissed at them, threatening mayhem. The sudden overpowering stench of burnt sage blew towards them.

Rod's black stripe of ashen ground angled slightly towards the fire, giving the fire a slight chance of passing between the two soot zones, if nothing were done about it. Already the flames surged nearer, and the bulge in the fire line, created by the sagebrush pointed straight at the gap. The wind shifted again, suddenly blowing towards them, and all at once Jake had a blinding haze of gray and white smoke in his face. He blinked his red eyes and turned his head.

He coughed, struck the new flare, and ran up, into the gap. Rod, striking his second flare as he ran, came from the other side. Jake started his next backfire, ran a few steps, and started another. He could barely see and could hardly breathe, but he didn't dare back off. With the wind pushing towards them, the house was in more danger than ever.

The two men met in the middle. Jake threw his flare upwind of him, into the now narrow strip of dry grass between the backfires and the advancing flames. Rod, after lighting one more backfire, did the same.

The wind shifted again, this time to the east, and the blaze that had been racing towards the backfires now turned parallel to them. The smoke cleared from Jake's eyes, if not from his lungs. His eyes still burned, and it was hard to see through the water dripping from his reddened eyelids, but he moved across the burn to the near edge, and began stamping his feet at anything that glowed.

"So," shouted Rod, "Suppose that I accept that your god-man is neither a legend nor a lama. What stops me from believing that he was insane?"

"Have you ever met someone who was truly delusional?" asked Jake, shouting back over the crackling of the straw. "It's pretty obvious, even if they're just slightly delusional. They say things that you know can't possibly be true."

"Do you know many delusional people?"

"In my line of work, I've counseled a few," said Jake. "One told me, with a calm matter-of-fact demeanor and with perfect sincerity, that his wife had a lover who snuck over at night and drilled screws into his tires."

"Did she?"

"Of course not. He worked night shifts in the warehouse of a hardware store. He ran over screws every time he went to work. They were all over the parking lot."

"So you're saying that your Jesus was like that?"

A spark from the sagebrush soared over Jake's head, landing on the inside of the firebreak. He ran and stomped it before it could blossom into flame.

"No, that's a very mild delusion," he shouted to Rod. "I'm saying that if Jesus was delusional, he was a million times worse than that. If He truly just believed that He was God, but He really wasn't, He'd – as C.S. Lewis put it, he'd be like a man who thinks he's a poached egg."

The two men were moving farther apart as they stamped, and Rod's reply was muffled by the wind. Jake kept treading, trying to blink away his tears as he did. He was afraid he might miss a spot, and let all their work go to waste. Then again, with his eyes watering so badly, his tears alone might put out the fire.

After a few more minutes, he was fairly sure that he had turned a corner, and was now stamping his earlier burn. He wiped his eyes on his shirt sleeve and turned in a circle, scanning the firebreak. Rod had just met up with his prior line of ash, and was now trotting back towards Jake.

In that direction, the firebreak touched the edge of the cliff. The fire could not flank them to the right. To the left of his own efforts, Nata was joining a hastily-scratched path of dirt to the edge of his soot zone. At the far end of that meandering strip of bare dirt, Guthrie was feebly scraping the grass away, in an effort to join Ashton's circle of mist and wet grass.

Ashton had stepped a few paces to his own left, and was now soaking the near end of the windward slope. Rising air, pushed uphill as it came off the bay, now turned the cone of water into a fountain. Droplets flew over Ashton's head, most of them landing in the grass near the house.

Because of the adverse winds, a good part of the water merely turned in the breeze and came back down on him. He kept raising the hose higher, in hopes of spraying it farther, but the resulting spindrift was mostly falling on Guthrie.

At least, thought Jake, *It's unlikely that Ashton or Guthrie is will catch fire.*

With her work done, Nata pulled a fresh flare from her pocket and struck it. She tossed it, underhand, into the grass a few feet from Guthrie. It landed in a dry patch, just outside Ashton's circle of dampness. The straw ignited and leaped up in flames, sending sparks into the air.

Guthrie jumped back, across the path, raising his shovel over his head, as if to beat the new fire into submission. He didn't have to; on touching the dirt streak, the fire turned and ran towards Jake. Soon the entire patch upwind of the dirt was nothing but soot, from Ashton to Jake. With little chance of moving against the wind, the backfire sputtered out.

Hot from the fire and the effort, Jake could feel the soot and grit on his face. He thought of running through the spray to cool himself, rinse his face, and check on the windward slope, but he knew better. It was dangerous.

Navy fire doctrine had taught him never to spray one of the firefighting team. If the fire grew too hot, the person could be badly burned as the water flashed to steam. Anyone who was accidentally sprayed by a fire hose had to be kept wet until the fire was out, or until he could be safely withdrawn.

Guthrie, now that he was wet, would need to be pulled back from the fire line. Or Ashton would have to keep him in the spray, which would be annoying to Guthrie. If Jake were to run through the mist, his firefighting would be over, as well.

It wasn't an idle threat. As the damage control chief had repeated endlessly aboard Jake's ship, navy fire doctrine existed because people had died doing things a different way. There were times for creativity, but firefighting wasn't one of them.

Instead Jake carefully made a wide circle behind the firebreak, moving around Marcion, and far to the left of Ashton. As the windward slope came into view, he smiled to himself. The wind was doing his job for him; at least in part. When it shifted and came from the north, it drove the fire towards the house, allowing the flames to burn down a small ways down the slope.

But then, when it shifted to come from the west again, those same flames were blown back up the hill, trapping the fire against the hillside. It could only burn into the pocket that they had created, and the fuel would be exhausted when it reached the eastward cut. Already the nearest advances of the grassfire were sizzling at the edge of Ashton's circle. The more easterly edge of the fire was now running along the border of the firebreak, reducing the small unburned patch to a triangle, then a pennant, and finally to nothing at all.

Fire still smoldered on the windward slope, but with adverse wind and what little moisture remained in the grass, it was finding the going tough. Jake walked wearily past the limits of Ashton's splash zone and began to stomp the edge of the fire, slowly walking it back towards its point of origin. Rod and Nata fell in line behind him, stomping anything that escaped the notice of his watery eyes.

Soon their stomping raised more red dirt than black ash. The fire was out, and the heroes, thoroughly dusted with fine soot and red dust that clung stubbornly to their sweaty skin and filled their pores, made their way back towards the house. It was only then, as the adrenaline abated, that they began to feel the strain from their efforts.

Guthrie, breathless, leaned on his shovel and panted like a dog that had just finished leading the pack in the Iditarod. Sweat from his bald brow had run across the soot on his forehead, making clean stripes down his ash-stained face. For a moment, he seemed like a valiant Pict, having defeated his enemies in battle; moments later, he resembled an old coal miner in a sprinkling rain.

Ashton, dripping with the water he had wasted, twisted the nozzle closed. Of all of them, he was the cleanest, but also the wettest. He gave the vague impression of a spectator at a killer whale show. He shivered in the breeze.

Rod, Nata, and Jake, trudging back downwind towards the house, could have been cast as a team of intrepid explorers who were finally reaching a remote waypoint in the Serengeti.

For the most minute of moments, they were one team, united in the common effort. Having a common goal had made them friends, it appeared, and Jake began to understand the bond between those who fought together in war.

Jake smiled and scanned the crew. The speech from the play about Henry the Fifth came to mind. And then the effect was broken. Marcion scowled at them all. "You're not all coming in here looking like that," she said.

Chapter Thirteen

FRESHLY SHOWERED AND CHANGED, Jake made his way down the stairs. Nata, the last one waiting for a turn, passed him by the doorway.

"I hope you left some hot water," she said.

"I did a navy shower," he said. "Five minutes, with stops for lathering. There should be plenty left."

"I suppose it's a fair question," said Rod, who sat on a divan in his bathrobe, rubbing his hair with a small towel. "Where does the hot water come from?"

"The water heaters are all propane-fired," said Guthrie. "The tanks are down by the dock."

"They couldn't have made the kitchen stove propane-fired as well?" asked Rod. "It would be a lot easy to use."

"I understand that it's more expensive that way. Something to do with the cost of running extra pipes all the way up the hill. Also, we wanted the place to look like it might be Edwardian."

Jake had not thought to bring a hairbrush, so he merely smoothed the hair across the top of his head with his bare hands. It still felt snarled and tangled, but he felt a little bit less like Frankenstein's monster.

"So, Jake, how do we know," said Rod, as Jake took a seat near him, "That this alpaca-preacher of yours really wasn't as crazy as a man who thinks he's a poached egg? If we take your gospels at face value, this man raved about the second temple being destroyed, threw odd curses at fig trees, and got into shouting matches with the authorities – the Pharisees and their lot: Called them vipers and whitewashed tombs, and all that."

"First, historically, the second temple really was destroyed, not long after he said all that about it happening. Forty years, at the outside, depending on how you date His life."

"*Post hoc ergo propter hoc,*" said Rod. "Did the Berlin wall come down because Reagan demanded it in 1987, or were the forces already in motion that would bring about the velvet revolution? It's the same kind of thing; it could be coincidence."

"If I say it will rain tomorrow, and the sky is clear now, but it rains tomorrow, it's a very reasonable inference that I knew something that you didn't know. It's the same with Jesus and his talk on the temple being destroyed. The disciples thought he was crazy, but the fact that He was right makes it reasonable to think he knew some inside information."

"Even a blind monkey gets a banana once in a while," said Rod. "Surprising, intriguing, but miraculous? Anyway, what else tells you that He wasn't crazy?"

"Will you, *ad argumentum*, consider the gospels as at least a guide to what Jesus said in them? It's what his followers said, sure; but they were the ones who knew Him best."

"I suppose that's fair, as you say, for discussion purposes. If we wanted to know what kinds of things Mohammad used to say, we'd look in the claims of his followers; the hadith, and all that. So, sure, *ad argumentum.*"

"Okay, then, as an example, take the famous sermon on the mount: in it He tells the people to be content with what they have, not to worry about things over which they have no control, and not to be upset when people call them names.

"He tells them that the eye is the lamp of the soul — the word picture has the mind as a room, with two windows for light. If the windows are dark, dirty, filtered through whatever evil you project onto the world, then your mind will also be dark and dingy. It will seem like a miserable place to be.

"If you want a clear mind, you need to see the world clearly, through clean eyes that see accurately, and let in good light. Not through your own lenses of anger and past pain. Not through darkened windows.

"He tells them not to be judgmental about others, and to concern themselves with resolving their own faults rather than seeing fault in others. He tells them that it's okay to be poor — it's not a sign of God's disfavor. It's okay to mourn, because in the end there's going to be comfort.

"Any clinician who works with the mind will tell her clients these exact same things — to see the world clearly, to focus on the immediate, to work on their own issues, and that depression doesn't last forever — days when a person feels horrible will be replaced by days when a person feels better."

"He probably never said those things at all," said Guthrie.

"Then Socrates probably never spoke a word, and Julius Caesar probably never went to Gaul," said Jake. "There's more manuscript support for the authenticity of the New Testament than for Plato or Julius Caesar put together."

"Alright, suppose he said all that," said Rod. "So maybe he ran hot and cold, like a cyclic disorder of some kind."

"People who are bipolar generally do not influence others for the better," said Jake. "Look at the Gadarene demoniac. This guy was bedlam crazy. He attacked people, he refused to wear clothes, and he ran around through the graveyards howling at the moon. Jesus spoke to him and he was suddenly calm, wearing clothes, and speaking normally.

"That makes Jesus the exact opposite of crazy. If He were crazy enough to think himself God, when He really wasn't, he and the Gadarene would have both been out there howling at the moon, and fighting over who did it better."

"You've snuck your bible in the back door," said Guthrie. "Jesus wasn't crazy because the bible tells me so."

"We're taking the most detailed accounts available to us," said Jake, "And that actually works against me in this case. There is certainly nothing at all in the any of the extra-biblical accounts to suggest that Jesus could have been crazy."

"You think any of this means anything?" asked Guthrie. "It's all just hand-waving and hypothesizing. You say that Jesus was God because He said that he was? Watch this. I, Carlisle Guthrie, am God incarnate." He turned to Jake. "There, does that make me God?"

"No," said Rod, wearily. "It makes you a liar. You are not God, and you don't believe you are. That eliminates two of the three choices – so you are a liar."

"So's his God," said Guthrie.

"Worthy of discussion," said Rod. "What stops Jesus from being a complete liar?"

Nata came back to the parlor, wearing pajamas, slippers, and a long towel that wrapped around her hair like a turban. She sat down by Rod. "What are we discussing?" she asked.

"More of their nonsense about that alpaca-God of his," said Guthrie. He looked over at Ashton, who was sound asleep from his exertions. "Where's Marcion?"

"She took to bed, claiming the exertion had exhausted her frail constitution. She said she didn't care if someone murdered her in her sleep, but if anyone does, it will be all of our faults."

"Of course," said Rod.

"Pity we don't have a servant who could make a hot drink. Not that coffee from earlier; it tasted like more like charcoal," said Guthrie. "I may never be able to fully get that awful taste out of my mouth."

"I believe I saw hot cocoa powder in the kitchen," Nata. "I suppose it's my turn to be the butler."

"There's a good point," said Guthrie. "What if the eighth pie was meant for a servant who stayed behind on the island? That would explain everything. What if it was that servant who killed Ulysses, tried to kill Jacobs, and set fire to the grass? That would be quite a pickle! Hard to say why; one never knows why people do things. Ah! And what if he or she is, even now, creeping up the stairs to do in Doctor Marcion?"

"Good riddance," said Ashton, softly, without opening his eyes. "We probably shouldn't interrupt him until he's had lots of time to finish." He paused. "Did I say that out loud?"

"I think we can rule it out," said Jake, "For the same reason we eliminated an eighth guest. Where would he sleep?"

"Well, there's that," said Guthrie, in a tone that suggested disappointment. "Besides, if we had a servant we'd have some food to eat. I'm starving."

Rod sighed. Nata got up and walked into the kitchen.

"So, Jake," said Rod. "What if this God business was a lie that got badly out of hand? We could understand it, surely: He wants to comfort people, like the sisters of Lazarus. So He says the first thing that pops into His head: I'm going to fix this. If I have to I'll, I'll, I'll raise your brother from the dead.

"And that gets transmuted in the telling and retelling into that bit about the resurrection and the life; no man who believes, and so on. From there it spins up; Someone says that he did raise Lazarus, someone else says they heard that he himself was raised by God, and on it goes. Just a mistake."

"That would be a pretty foolish mistake. Also, one thing we see about Jesus through all the gospels is that he wasn't one to give in to social pressure. He did the right thing, always, even when it was the weird thing, or the unpopular thing."

"So he wouldn't have tried to comfort the sisters? This is where that verse is found, after all, about how He wept."

"Not by lying to them. Jesus' teachings were hard. They were firm, emphatic, even harsh. He was compassionate and kind, but never at the expense of the truth."

"You seem to be pinning a lot on how well you think you know His personality, just from reading his friends' accounts of Him. That seems like a bit of a stretch. It would be like me thinking I knew the mind of Sherlock Holmes from reading

Arthur Conan Doyle. Or that I was an expert on the mind of Lord Peter Wimsey because I'd read my Sayers."

"Alright," said Jake, "So where does that leave us? If you think He might, from kindness, tell a lie like that, knowing that the people around Him were going to invest their lives in it and die for it, then you're stuck between the last two ells, Liar or Lord. I guess, if nothing else will serve, we can decide between those based on whether He did what He said."

"You mean scouring the gospels to verify his actions? Dig into archaeology for his fingerprints on stones?"

"No, we really just need to verify the one huge claim in particular. He didn't just claim He was God. He claimed He'd prove it, and that he would personally rise from the dead on the third day."

"Did he really say that? Maybe that's written back into his legend by his gospel-writing friends."

Nata returned with cocoa. She left a large mug by Ashton's elbow, handed one to Guthrie, put two on the coffee table between Jake and Rod, and then settled onto a divan, pulling a blanket over herself.

"I put the two mugs between you so that you can choose between them yourselves," she said. "It occurred to me that if I were the killer, you might be putting too much trust in me."

"And what if you poisoned all the mugs?" asked Rod.

Guthrie swallowed hard and choked on his cocoa, but managed to put it down without either spilling or spraying the room. "Did you?" he asked.

"No," she said, with a grin. "But you can swap mugs with Ashton if you're nervous."

Jake picked up a mug. "I'll go with this one," he said. "I have no worries over it."

"Maybe there's a code between you, to tell Jacobs which mug is safe," said Guthrie. "Don't take that other mug, Rod."

"I'll taste both of them if it makes you feel any better," said Jake. "None of the mugs are poisoned."

"How can you be certain?" asked Rod, picking up his mug and tasting it. "I'm sure that I would not recognize belladonna if it bit me. Or if I drank it."

"Logic," said Jake. "It's a powerful tool."

"It is indeed," said Rod. "And you've proven to yourself that Nata didn't just kill us. I'll trust your logic that far. But you haven't proven to me, or to anyone, that Jesus didn't lie to Mary and Martha." He drank deep from his mug. "Very nice," he said. "The cocoa, I mean."

"It'll do," said Guthrie.

"The single most important claim Jesus ever made was that He would rise from the dead."

"Are we sure he said that?"

"As sure as we can be on historical facts," said Jake. "For one thing, as I said before, we see the witnesses at His first trial claiming that he said He would destroy the temple. But that's not quite what he said. He claimed that it they were to destroy His temple – His body – He would rebuild it in three days."

"So they got it wrong," said Guthrie.

"If the gospels were a propaganda piece, they would have said it correctly. The writers would have wanted to reinforce the correct message, and never give the readers even the slightest chance to misunderstand. So the misstatement – that He said He would destroy the temple - must be accurately recorded."

"A stretch," said Rod.

"Criterion of embarrassment," said Nata. "When a person claims a thing which casts a bad light, it is more likely to be true. So the idea that these witnesses misunderstood Jesus is more likely a historical fact. Like in Acts 25, where Festus says that Paul's in jail for saying that a dead man is alive."

She shook her head. "I'm not sure which is stranger: that I remember that passage, or that all of a sudden I'm arguing for the wrong side. What's in this cocoa?"

"I'd call it more of a statement against interest," said Rod. "But I'll grant it for the moment."

130

"So it all hinges, then, on whether He did rise from the dead." Jake drank some cocoa, and wiped his mouth with the small towel draped over his shoulder.

"How exactly do we settle that question?" asked Rod. "It seems to me that people have been trying to answer it since he died. And yet it's still in question."

He looked around. "And speaking of that... Would you and Nata step outside with me for a moment? I saw something odd and I want your opinion about it. Opinions; both of you."

"I suppose we should check for a reflash," said Jake. "The fire flaring back up again. The Navy would have expected us to set a watch."

"*Flaring* back up?" Nata shook her head. "Only you, Jake."

Guthrie was already settling himself into his chair for a nap, and drawing a quilt over his torso. Ashton had returned to a state indistinguishable from sleep, except for the odd snore from time to time. Nata and Jake stood, and followed Rod out through the kitchen.

The box of fusees had not chosen to escape again, and the blue tarp folded on top of the box fluttered in the breeze. Rod led them down the path that Nata and Guthrie had scraped, then onto the burn that he and Jake had made. Each step raised a puff of powdered ash.

As they approached the eastward cut, Rod stopped and pointed. Just on the leeward side of the burn, there was a small pit, and dirt had been piled on a tarp beside the hole. It was mostly round, unevenly dug, perhaps two feet deep, and about four feet in diameter. It seemed to have been very hastily made.

It was in a small natural depression, and near the house. Jake hadn't seen it until they were right on top of it. One window of the sitting room faced towards the pit, but heavy black curtains prevented them from seeing into the house. It was debatable in Jake's mind if the pit would have been visible from inside. *A moot point,* he decided.

"Not long enough for a grave," said Nata.

"Barely a meter across," said Rod. "But perhaps, if it were deeper, one might place a body into a fetal position."

"But where is the body?" asked Nata.

"And what interrupted the digging?" asked Jake.

"The fire, perhaps?" posed Rod.

"No," said Jake. "We were all inside, and accounted for, when we saw the fire."

"Daylight?" asked Nata. "The person responsible for this was probably the person from last night who stabbed you and knocked me out."

"Digging in the dark seems very risky," said Jake.

"Especially so near the edge," said Nata, eyeing the nearby cliff. "One might never be seen again."

"Once one has undertaken murder, perhaps then one is filled with a reckless disregard for one's own safety," said Rod.

"There might be something to that: Exposure to one's fears changing one's anxiety levels," said Jake, stepping around Nata, stopping between her and the edge. "I've heard it said that skydiving significantly lessens one's fear of heights. But we probably should move back inside, before we're missed."

"One word of caution," said Rod. "I've shown this to you because the two of you seem to be sensible. The others might be alarmed by this. We wouldn't want them to panic."

"We certainly wouldn't," said Jake.

"If the killer knows that we know, he might decide to do something drastic." She pantomimed being stabbed.

"A rule that I learned long ago, playing chess," said Jake, "Is to never to assume that the opponent doesn't see and know the same things that you do." He gestured towards the path, and Nata started walking that way.

Back inside, they settled into chairs, as before.

"Before our little field trip, you were about to prove the resurrection," said Rod. "No doubt by vaguely appealing to the conversion of St. Paul."

"That's not the only evidence," said Jake. "I understand that Gary Habermas is currently writing a multi-volume work on the evidence for the resurrection."

He was interrupted by a pounding at the door. They all looked at each other.

"I guess the pizza's here," said Rod.

"Did Marcion go for a hike and lock herself out?" asked Nata. "That would be just like her. Except for the hiking."

"I'll go and see," said Jake. The huge door shook with the fervent pounding of fists. "Coming!"

He was back in a moment, with a small Vietnamese man in tow. The man seemed highly distressed, and badly puzzled. Jake smiled at the duo and gestured towards the man.

"Nata, Rod, I'd like you to meet one of the deacons from my church. This is Nguyen Chi Due." Chi Due bowed slightly. Rod stood and offered a hand, with Chi Due shook weakly.

"Xin chao, ahn Chi Due," said Nata, with a faint nod of her head. She seemed about to laugh at the incongruity.

"Em xin chao," said Chi Due.

"Has he been here this whole time?" asked Rod, with a grin. "Was that the clue? Was the eighth pie for him?"

"No, he has just arrived," said Jake. "And he brought a fishing boat with him." He turned to Chi Due. "You saw the smoke, no doubt."

"Yes, there was big cloud, lots of smoke. My wife sent me to look for you. Bryly, she was very worried. I saw smoke, on this island; I said, this will be the place. We find – found, we found the dock. I came up; they wait for me at the dock."

"Will your boat carry six?" asked Jake.

"No, Pastor, I have two men, plus we caught lot of fish. It is small boat, a small boat."

"It seems that we're back to that fox and chicken riddle," said Nata. "And we're not even sure which one of us is the kungfu chicken."

"Is suspect that those two are the bags of grain," said Rod, gesturing to Ashton and Guthrie.

"I may have a solution," said Jake. "I'll have Chi Due, and his crew, run over to the mainland. They'll bring back help for the rest of us. Meanwhile, There's something I'll have him take back. Don't get up; I'll be back momentarily."

Jake turned to the small deacon. "Would you mind calling your crew up here? We may need more people."

Chi Due said something in Vietnamese, into a small radio. A moment later, there was a flurry of words. "They will meet us," he said.

"Tell them to meet us past the house, on the leeward side, close to the cliff," said Jake.

There was more radio chatter, and the Chi Due followed him out through the kitchen. Rod and Nata stared after them for a moment, and then resumed their discussion.

When the other two men reached them, they were standing by the ersatz grave. Jake took one corner of the tarp and looked at Chi Due, who took the next corner. Then they both walked past the hole, letting the tarp tilt its dirt into the pit.

The dirt was heavier than Jake had expected, but they pulled slowly, letting the dirt pour down the edge, into the hole. When the tarp had lightened enough, they stepped past the pit, inverting the tarp.

Beneath the spot where the tarp had lain were Ulysses and the peppermill.

Chapter Fourteen

CHI DUE'S MEN RECOILED in horror. Chi Due turned around when he heard them gasp, then took a sudden step back in shock and dismay.

"Ah, Pastor Jake! What have you done?"

The other two men exchanged whispers and murmurs in Vietnamese, looking from the body to Jake, and back again. Chi Due made a gesture to them, and they stopped.

"I assure you, I didn't do this," said Jake. "But someone has, and if they have a chance, they will steal this body and hide it again. Can you take it with you? Call the police as soon as you're in Richmond, and tell them everything."

"Everything, just like what I see?"

"Yes, including that there are six people trapped on this island. Tell them to send the ferry."

There followed an argument in Vietnamese, which Jake did not follow in the least. Well, there did appear, from the hand gestures, to be some doubts about Jake's character, and some comments about the offensive odor from the body. Or that was

Jake's impression, based mainly on reading their faces and their gestures. At one point in the discussion, the two men stared at Jake and took a step away from him.

At the end of the argument, Ulysses was rolled tightly into the tarp. The two men lifted him with some difficulty, and then carried him away. Chi Due shook Jake's hand once more, and ran after his crew.

Jake went back into the house, stopping in the kitchen to wash his hands. As he came back out to the parlor, Rod and Nata were chatting. Nata laughed at something.

"Just in time," said Nata. "Rod was regaling me with tales of his adventures in Prague. I'll have to visit there some day."

"I presume that we shall be rescued soon," said Rod. "Since we didn't all climb onto the small boat."

"I'm going to say forty-five minutes or an hour, round trip, allowing time to arrange the ferry and all," said Jake.

"I don't suppose we should wake the others yet," said Rod. "I'm finding myself a bit weary of their company."

"You're very polite," said Nata.

"Since we have so little time, we must perhaps rush the main course," said Rod. "So tell us how you claim to know that the resurrection truly happened. After all, it is the great decider between the last two ells."

"You mentioned the conversion of Paul," said Jake. "And you're right, that's definitely one of my go-to arguments for the resurrection. Also the birth of the church, the change in the disciples, the conversion of James the Just, the rapid creation of the pre-Pauline creed, and sometimes I throw in the Lithuanian argument, just for a change."

"That one sounds rather Baltic," said Nata.

"It's good, but with the time crunch, we probably should look at Paul. So here is Rabbi Shaul, an up-and-coming young Pharisee, with his whole life ahead of him.

"He has a good family, he is a Roman citizen by birth, he's a student of the great Gamaliel, whom some say is second only to Hillel in wisdom and knowledge. He's a made man, and the world is at his feet. He's in the holy city of his people, and what does he hear as he walks down the street?

"Blasphemy. There's a guy right there in the street arguing with the teachers and the scribes, telling them that they are guilty of the blood of Jesus, the Messiah. He stops to see this spectacle, and before he knows it, people are asking him to hold their coats while they stone this blasphemer. That would be Stephen, the deacon, of course."

Jake picked up his mug. "Was this one mine?"

"It doesn't matter," said Nata. "I didn't actually poison any of them. I wouldn't really know how."

He sipped the cocoa. "So where were – Ah, right. So Shaul becomes a great enemy of this new sect that is rising, the Sect of the Way. It all seems to hinge on some teacher who got himself crucified, and whom His followers say was the Messiah, and rose from the dead."

"That would be the evil superstition of which Tacitus and Suetonius would later speak."

"Precisely. Shaul becomes fanatical about tracking these guys down, getting them arrested, and killing them when he can. He's ruthless. I mean, imagine it: This crucified man – It would be like a death-row convict, to us, today, or worse – and these Christians have the audacity to say that this criminal is God.

"Then one day, Saul sees a vision, and he makes a complete about-face. He drops everything, throws his life away, and becomes one of the leaders of this new sect."

"Could have been a hallucination," said Rod. "Or a seizure. I think Luke said it was a hot day, they'd been walking in the sun – Heat stroke?"

"That's been proposed, but it won't wash out. Let's put a pin in that and come back to it. He makes a big life change, and that's the point." He finished the cocoa in the mug. "He was fairly well off; now he's broke. He was a Pharisee, now he's nobody. He would have eventually become a great teacher, maybe even the high priest. Well, no, he was from Benjamin, not Levi, so that wouldn't work.

"But he lost his fortune, his friends, his family, his career, and for what? Going back to that seizure idea… Or heat stroke … I might accept that if he wasn't such a scholar. This is a guy who knows the Tanakh—"

"Sorry, the what?" asked Rod.

"What we Christians call the Old Testament. To him, it would have been called the Tanakh, an acronym for the Law, the Prophets, and the Writings."

"Anyway," said Nata.

"Anyway, he wouldn't have changed religions easily. He was pretty well rooted in Judaism. So, let's say it was just a hallucination. Well, once he got his bearings again, he'd have known it wasn't Jesus speaking to him. He'd have found a way to reconcile it with his current faith."

"He did seem to be given to dreams and visions," said Nata. "The Macedonian dream, for example. Or being caught up into the third heaven."

"Persistent hallucinations don't work like that," said Jake. "I've talked to Bryly about this – she's a mental health clinician – and I'm pretty sure that if Paul had a mental condition, he would not have been able to write the way that he did.

"His letters are models of style and structure. They have a clear outline, they move from point to point in a linear fashion, they answer likely objections by an interlocutor – Take Romans. It's a very clear discussion of the mechanics of salvation, which is a deep topic, but Paul makes it simple and straightforward. Even if it wasn't important for Christians, it would be good literature. On the order of Marcus Aurelius, or even Socrates.

"So he wasn't crazy. He wasn't the sort of guy who stands on a street corner and shouts at passing cars. Which is kinda the crazy he would have to be."

"Maybe he was simply wrong," said Rod.

"But he knew better," said Jake. "I'm of the opinion that Barnabus wrote Hebrews, but suppose for a moment it was Paul. At the very least, the tone and theology is very like Paul, and the writer knew him. That book makes it clear that once you leave the Jewish religion, there's no turning back. That would have been the theological position of Paul's circle.

"And that joins in with all Paul's letters. He knew the law, and he rejected it in favor of salvation by grace. It's not that he was duped by a clever parlor trick. Once he asked himself if it really could be true – if Jesus could actually be the Messiah – all the pieces fell into place. The Tanakh opened itself up to him and said, 'Look, I told you so.' He finally got it."

"I am not a clinician," ceded Rod. "So I cannot fairly judge the apostle's sanity."

"Let's just agree on this part, then: From his writings, he doesn't sound crazy. Fair enough?"

"Fair enough. But does it prove the resurrection?"

"It certainly points to it," said Jake. "But as we look at more evidence, the case gets stronger."

"I want to hear about the Lithuanian thing," said Nata.

"Okay. I have a friend who wrote a book on Easter, and one of his arguments goes like this: Suppose that there was a new religious leader who rose up in Vilnius, around 1776 or so."

"I don't know where that is," said Nata.

"Capital of Lithuania," said Rod. "Go on."

"Well, Lithuania is to America like Judea would have been to the Roman Empire. In terms of population, proportionately, you understand, and in terms of things like trade. Probably a bit less significant, because it's not a path into the middle east, or a territory of the United States, or anything like that."

"Ah, so this man is an analog for Christ, and Lithuania is to America like Judea would be to Romans. Somewhere way off over there, so to speak."

"An analogy, yes. Suppose, for example, that, like Christ, this man never leaves the area around Vilnius, never writes anything, never makes any art, and never runs for any political office. He is actively teaching for only about three years, and then is tried on false charges and executed by the government.

"You'd never hear about this guy, right? Really, how much do you know about Lithuania at all?"

The other two shrugged.

"Right," continued Jake. "But by about 1805, let's say, while Stephan Decatur is in the Mediterranean, fighting off the Barbary pirates, there is so much rioting in Washington about this one guy from Vilnius, that the president has to eject all the Lithuanians from Washington."

"Were there even Lithuanians in Washington then?"

"Let's suppose that there were."

"I think I remember this," said Nata. "In Acts, there's a couple of Jewish Christians who were ejected from Rome."

"Suetonius mentions it, and I think some others. It may have happened up to three times during Claudius' reign. Within twenty or thirty years after the crucifixion."

"Live and learn," said Rod. "Interesting thought."

"Now fast forward to today, and suppose that the religion that has grown up around this obscure Lithuanian guy – His followers claim he rose from the dead – is now the single largest sect in America, and people meet every Sunday to sing to this guy. The President even tries to make it the state religion."

"You can't do that," said Nata.

"Right, but some 300 years after Christ, Constantine did exactly that. Do you get how improbable it is that one teacher from Judea, who only taught for three years, could create a religion that was the single largest sect in the Roman Empire 300 years later? How does that happen without there being something very significant about this man and his teachings?"

"What is this book?" asked Rod. "The one where you said that you found this argument?"

"It's called *Easter, Fact or Fiction*, by Chase A. Thompson," said Jake. "He's a pastor at a church across town from me."

"Okay, I'm not entirely convinced," said Rod. "But you do make a strong case. I'll need to think about these things. What is your church again?"

"I'm at Central Baptist Church, on Alabama Street, in Salinas," said Jake. "If you're ever down our way, call me. Or drop by. I'd like to discuss a few things with you, once this is all over. A few questions, mainly, which probably wouldn't be best until after we're back on the mainland."

"I doubt I will," said Rod. "But it was a good discussion. For not being a Jesuit, you've proved most interesting." He offered his hand, and Jake shook it.

"I try to be entertaining," said Jake.

Ashton made a particularly distressing snore.

"I suppose we should wake them and herd them down to the dock," said Nata, nodding to Guthrie and Ashton.

"We need to alert someone to the missing body and the shallow grave by the burn," said Rod. "Will the police send over a helicopter for it, do you think?"

"The police already have the body," said Jake.

"Well, that's quite the rabbit," said Nata, "And you don't even have a hat. Where was it?"

"Under the tarp, beneath the pile of dirt."

"How did you kn– how could you possibly have known that?" asked Rod, with a grin.

"It seemed likely," said Jake. "Why would the killer stop digging? Well, no good reason I could think of – unless the empty shallow grave was what he had intended to make in the first place. Why would he want a shallow grave? As a reason to have dirt piled beside it." Jake shrugged. "And there he was."

"Remind me never to play chess against you," said Rod.

Chapter Fifteen

ROD AND JAKE STOOD alone at the back rail of the blue and white boat as it puttered towards the shore. It might have been the one that brought them, though it seemed to Jake that the colors were slightly different.

The benches were still hard, worn, and not designed for anything approaching comfort. None of the six passengers had chosen to make use of them.

The bay was clear now, and Jake could see the towering spires on the far peninsula. To the south, the bay bridge reached out across the calm blue water. To the west, despite the glare of the sun on the water, Jake thought he saw the golden gate bridge. To the north was the tiny island that had so recently been their prison.

"I am disappointed, Jake, that we reached the end of our stay without finding the murderer," said Rod, with a smirk.

"Oh, I knew all along who killed Ulysses. It was you."

"What? That's ridiculous! Why would you possibly believe such a thing?"

"Well, philosophically speaking, you are the only one who could have done such a thing, and then could have calmly eaten breakfast in the adjoining room. The others would have been agitated, or else would have stayed silent to hide their guilt. But you could rationalize it."

"What motive could I possibly have? I never met the man before this little excursion."

"You gave your motive away when you said that you would play the *teufel-advokat*. You are obviously an imposter.

"Those are not Czech words. *Teufel* is German, and *advokat* is not. It belongs to the northern Germanic languages, such as Norse, Swedish, or Danish, but it might be borrowed into Czech. A German would say a *teufel-anwalt;* a true Czech would say a *d'abluv advokat*. Only a German pretending to be Czech would blend the words like that.

"That means that you're not Dr. Dobrazamery. But you've been in a place where many languages are spoken, poorly, and where they tend to get jumbled into a patois of sorts. Like naval service, or time spent in a prison.

"Having a look in Ulysses' room confirmed it: He had the real Dobrazamery's book, and from it, he knew that you were not him. So he had to die. And he did."

"An intriguing theory, but I assure you, I am most certainly Rodel Dobrazamery. I can show you my passport, my papers."

"You have to say so, of course. And you are probably close enough in appearance for the passport to match up. But you're clearly not a medical doctor, for one thing. Your clever sense of humor betrays you. Doctors are trained to be serious and literal.

"If I tell my wife that I have a lump in my throat, she will hug me for being in touch with my feelings. If I say that same phrase to my doctor, he will palpate my submandibular lymph nodes. My wife often jokes that in the first year of medical school, all the doctors' funny-bones are removed, and from then on, nothing is humerus."

"So doctors are not smart enough?"

"They're smart, but they can't ever assume anything to be a joke. They can't risk being wrong – taking a serious symptom as a joke. So they play it safe."

"Was it just that? My sense of humor?"

"Well, that and other small things: Your hands are warm and your handshake is firm. A doctor's hands are almost always smooth, soft and cool, from their well-known habits of copious handwashing and sanitizing."

"That seems like a hasty generalization."

"Perhaps. Tell me if you ever find an exception. I never have. But we digress. I suspect that you are either a fugitive or a former convict of some sort. You must have just happened to encounter Dobrazamery on the way to the airport, killed him, and took his identity. With his papers, ticket, and passport, you were safely out of the country, and ready to assume a new life. No one here knew you, so it worked, for a while.

"Dobrazamery was on his way here, to this gathering. You figured that it couldn't hurt to play along: Meals, a hiding place, and a chance for a good discussion on your favorite topics.

"But by chance, Ulysses had Dobrazamery's book. I didn't see a photo on the back cover, but something made it obvious to him that you weren't the doctor. Then, in turn, he must have said something that tipped you off that he knew. Maybe you laughed at his joke; maybe he even accused you.

"You came downstairs later and found him asleep in a chair in the drawing room. There would be blood on the carpet if you killed him there, so you lured him into the kitchen with the promise of more chicken cobbler. You may have eaten the eighth one in front of him, as bait. We were all hungry; it would have worked for me."

Rod smiled and flushed slightly, but said nothing.

"In the kitchen," said Jake, "You clobbered him with the large peppermill, but then you heard footsteps. That would have been me. So you turned out the light and hid in the closet. The peppermill rolled under the table, where I found it later."

"A nice speculation," said Rod, "And clever in its way."

"And entirely correct, isn't it?" Jake shook his head. "What had me stumped was how you got past me to manage to be in your room when I awoke the rest. But a house built in this style

144

– especially if there were to be overnight occupancy – could not just have one stairwell. Sure enough, I found a back stairwell near the kitchen, ending in the maid's closets on each floor. You must have run up the stairs, and even then, you must have barely slipped into your room ahead of me."

"I think you were just at the foot of the stair," said Rod.

"Ah. I must have spent too long ruminating on the thump in the parlor. Was that you running for the back stairs?"

"Nope. I did find a vase fallen over when I got downstairs the next morning. I suspect a cat."

"Still, you didn't have long to hide the body before you were going to be under continuous observation. So I think that the body went into the kitchen closet."

"You've got me there. I managed to be the first down after you woke us. I finished cleaning up the kitchen then, and made sure the kitchen closet was closed, then dashed into the parlor and started crumpling newspaper for a fire. Lucky for me, you stopped to dress before coming back down. And in my haste, I missed the peppermill under the table."

"When we searched later, you checked that closet, as I recall, and even made note of the MREs stored there. That kept me from seeing the body. Later, you were the one who retrieved the MREs, which kept Nata from seeing the body."

"And thus I was able to gaslight you all a bit longer. Eventually, I had to do the tarp trick, or else he would have started to smell." He shrugged. "So why couldn't it have been Nata you suspected, with her raincoat still damp from dragging the body outside?"

"Well, partially my intuition: I knew her, as you recall. I couldn't see Lisa Bertrand killing in cold blood. In a fit of anger, well, maybe. But not in cold blood."

"And the other part that convinced you?"

"The goofy story about the cat. Marcion was right: No one else heard the meow. If she had gone for a walk in the fog, she would have just said so, and that would have been enough. And if the roof were leaking, she'd have placed a bucket, not donned a raincoat and stood under it. So she was out on the roof.

"The cat story was plausible, but just barely. It seemed like too much of a spur-of-the-moment story. But, again, I know Nata, from a long time ago, and I think I know why she was on the roof."

"Why would that be?"

"Penitent privilege applies," said Jake. "Her confessions and private matters are between us and God. I can only say that she didn't kill Ulysses. As for the others, none of them were physically capable of lifting and moving Ulysses' body. So even if your philosophy didn't point you out as the only one who could do it, abductive reasoning made it obvious."

"Abductive. So when you have eliminated the impossible?"

"Exactly. You had means, that is, you're one of the two of us who could lift the body. You had motive: To cover up your theft of Dobrazamery's identity. And you made an opportunity by enticing him with the eighth pie."

"What about the burned paper?"

"An obvious red herring. I saw through it at once. You were in the kitchen, presumably making coffee, though you hadn't made much progress by the time Nata and I went to clean her wound. You had time to write the note, burn the edges, and place it for its discovery. And then, with us there, you found it."

"That couldn't be a coincidence?"

"A clue that conveniently points to the least-liked member of our party? And that is proffered by my best suspect?" Jake shook his head. "You might as well have written out a signed confession. It merely confirmed what I already knew."

"Alright, Jake," said Rod, softly, "To you, just to you, I will confess it. What you have said is true. I was nominally Roman Catholic when I entered prison at Stadlheim. But my faith was not strong, not like yours. You would call me a Christmas-and-Easter kind of Christian.

"Within a couple of months, I gave it up entirely. Prisons in Bavaria are not like prisons here; they confine but they do not crush. There was a lot of discussion among us, and some of the prisoners with me were well-educated. It gave me a chance to explore my philosophies, to learn, to read. Having given up Christianity, I soon went to the polar opposite: Nihilism."

"From Rome to Carthage."

"Precisely. Why should we carry around the baggage of our religion if it is not actually true?"

"And it relieved you of guilt for your crimes."

"My conscience was never strong, but yes, as you say, I felt no remorse for my crimes, then or now," said Rod. "Including escaping the prison, and killing the Czech, in order to get out of Europe. By coincidence, my name truly is Rod, but from Roden instead of Rodel. When I found the doctor, and the name, and our slight resemblance, it just seemed like ... well, not fate, of course. But too good to pass up."

"And as a nihilist, you were able to be pragmatic about it."

"And about killing Ulysses, and about trying to stab you. It was not personal, of course; but still, I don't see how you could have anticipated that. I am quite impressed that you managed it. The trick with the pillow, that is."

"I didn't," said Jake. "I was as surprised as all the rest of them to see the knife there. It was luck— well, no, it was divine Providence that I was out sneaking around when you tried it."

"You don't seem very angry about it, either," remarked Rod. "I mean, for the knife and all. I did try to kill you in your sleep. I couldn't blame you if you wanted revenge."

"I can forgive it," said Jake. "You did what you felt you must, to try to wriggle out of the noose. It doesn't mean that I'll ever trust you around a sharp object in the future, but for the stabbing attempt, at least, I hold no ill will towards you. *Ego te absolvo.*" He held out his hand, and Rod shook it.

"That is more gracious than I deserve. I can only hope that when the boat reaches the dock at Richmond, that I can count on your discretion a little bit longer, in those other matters of which we spoke. Penitent privilege? Was that what you called it? When you cannot speak of what is confessed?"

"I cannot reasonably say that a dedicated atheist is relying upon me for religious advice, so you can't count on me there, I'm afraid. I will have to say what I know, and to explain my reasoning to the detective in charge.

"There will be police waiting at the dock, and they will likely keep us for hours on end. We can expect to make lengthy statements, and we can expect to be fingerprinted. When the fingerprints deny that you are Dobrazamery, your goose will be well and truly cooked. I won't lie for you. But I won't try to hold you for them when we get off the boat."

"Well and truly cooked," said Rod. "That's a nice phrase. Perhaps I'll run. Perhaps I'll confess. I don't know yet. But Jake, despite how things have turned out, it was a pleasure to meet you. We may cross paths again."

"Likewise, Rod. If you do happen to wind up in prison, drop me a line. I'll come and visit."

"I'd like that." He moved forward, leaving Jake at the rail.

Jake saw Nata by the port side rail and moved over next to her. She nodded to him, without ever taking her eyes off of the red island, jutting up like a lump of paprika.

"There was no cat, was there?" he asked.

"No. But I couldn't do it."

"I know. You weren't on the window sill when I knocked. You were by the door. You had to be; you opened it too fast. So you had already come back inside."

"You don't need to tell anyone," she said. "Don't make it into a thing. It was just a momentary lapse. Nothing more than that. I'm over it now."

"If you ever do it, I'll never forgive you."

"You can't say things like that this time. It's not the same. You're married now, with one on the way."

"I am. And I don't love you the way I did in high school. Now it's *phileo*, the love of brothers, or of family. Still, it would make me very angry to see you do what you were thinking."

"It's Tolstoy. It's his silly questions, always in my head. Is there something that I ought to be doing with my life, or, you know, accomplishing? And if so, what is it?"

"Tolstoy found an answer to those questions."

"I know that answer, the one you're thinking of, and don't know if I can go back there again. I'm not that same little girl any more. I don't know if that answer is big enough for me."

"That answer will always fit. It will grow to meet you where you are. When we were young, we understood big things in the simple ways, but that doesn't mean that those things were simple. It just means that we weren't aware of how deep they were. Call me when you're ready, and I'll see that you find your way. I can't push you there, but I can walk alongside you."

"This makes twice."

"I know. So you have good reason to think carefully about how very angry it would make me. You owe it to me."

"I see what you did there. You're trying to give me a good reason not to. It's emotional manipulation."

"I'm pretty transparent," said Jake. "It's a really good thing I don't play poker. I'd lose my shirt."

"And possibly your collar as well."

The boat nosed up to the dock, where three police cruisers lined the shore. Officers in uniform, and one in plain clothes, waited on the dock. As Jake watched, Rod stepped forward, offering them his wrists. He turned and nodded to Jake.

Bryly was also there, waving her arm to him. She held one arm low, around her belly. Seeing her was like a breath of fresh air in his face. He hadn't realized until then how stuffy and dull the island had been, without her. Even the boat seemed gloomy, now, in retrospect.

He hurried towards the brow, to meet her. A police officer stopped him and pointed him to a nearby building. He looked at Bryly and shrugged. She blew him a kiss, and waved.

That evening, Jake and Bryly sat on the couch. She had her shoulder blade nestled against his armpit, and his arm pulled around her like a blanket.

"I'm surprised," said Bryly, when he had told her the story, from train to reunion. "I thought all along that it would turn out to be Marcion. Or that snarky Guthrie fellow."

"People can be evil without being murderers," said Jake.

"But Rod? I mean, he was friendly and collegial."

"What did Shakespeare say? 'Meet it is I set it down: that a man may smile and smile…' "

" 'And be a villain.' Yes, I get it. But out of all of them, he seemed like a genuinely nice person, even with his Rome versus Carthage mentality. As a psychological clinician, I'm tempted to hand in my license. I still can't believe it."

"He was the only one who could have done it. All of the others felt that killing was morally wrong, even though they were atheists. As Rod put it, they wanted both the rules of Rome and the freedom from rules found only in Carthage."

"That makes no sense, to me, but I get it. People don't think their philosophies all the way through. And that is why I have a job, I suppose."

"But Rod did think it through. He saw, as I did, that for a moral basis, it's either Christ or nothing at all. It's not that an atheist can't be moral; it's that they have no reason to. So he could kill in cold blood, and feel no remorse at all. No one could hold him accountable, and there was, in his view, nothing wrong with what he did."

"You forgave him for trying to kill you?"

"As we both did with the Hoppemans, when they tried it."

"I'm proud of you. A man of grace."

"I like that title. I might put it on my business cards. Jake Jacobs, Pastor and International Man of Grace."

"International?"

"I went to Canada once."

"Ah. So what about the pocket watch?"

"Absolutely unrelated. Just a memento of his past."

150

"And the noise in the parlor?"

"Probably my imagination, but it might have been a cat. Or even an imperceptible earthquake. One of those 2.0 things that we have all the time, but nobody can even feel."

"That book with the ridiculous title?"

"Coincidence, or else Ulysses wanted to know more about his colleagues. Apparently he, alone of them all, lived there. The others merely visited."

"And why did Rod start the grassfire? What would be the point? He was in as much danger from it as the rest of you."

"Rod didn't start the fire."

"There were only three people on the island who knew how to start a fire," said Bryly. "So it was Nata?"

"Nope," said Jake.

"Jake! Why would you start a grassfire?"

"I didn't mean to," he said. "It was a side effect of flares. One of them rolled downhill, in spite of the little tab on its plastic cap. I might not have even put the cap back on."

"I suppose it was providential," said Bryly. "It brought Chi Due, and eventually it brought the police."

"And a gardening supplier from a nursery in Richmond."

"A gardening supplier?"

"When I went to the mine, I set up a small gas generator and a flashing light. I thought I rigged it to signal 'Send Rescue.' But as it happens, my Morse code is a bit rusty. It was sending 'Seed Fescue.' So, of course, the nursery thought I was placing an order, and they brought over grass seed."

"You're making that up. Jake Jacobs, you are lying to me, and right in front of little Faith. Oh, my goodness!" Her smile gave away that she was not actually angry.

"Sorry, Faith," said Jake. "Daddy was joking with Mommy. But that is no excuse for you to ever be less than truthful."

"Much better," she said. "We both need to make sure we set good examples for her now. And we need to start screening colleges soon."

"For this very moment, I am so looking forward to a good night's rest, without worrying about being stabbed or clubbed in my sleep." He looked at her with a speculative eye. "You do promise that you won't, right?"

"Somers really dumped you into it, didn't he?

"I suppose that I had it coming. We did all throw him under the bus at the ministerial breakfast that one time."

"So, one thing I still don't get: when did Rod go out and dig the fake grave?"

"I'm not sure. It might have been while I was playing chess against Nata. He was away for a little while then. But did he have time to put out the flares, hide the box, and then dig that grave? I don't think so."

"Could he have done it that night, while you were doing your nocturnal adventures?"

"I doubt it; he'd have seen me re-lighting the flares. I'd likely have gotten a shovel across my skull."

"That leads me to ask, when you were out skulking in the night, what else were you doing? You clearly found the flares, and re-lit the signal – So why didn't someone see that and send help? It was night time, after all, and the storm was over."

"I asked the Richmond police while they were questioning us. They said that they didn't get any calls from any motorists. Maybe it was just foggy enough that they only saw a fuzzy red light in the distance."

"Or maybe they were all on their phones. Do you know how many people I see driving... Well, never mind."

"For whatever reason, the flares didn't do the job."

"How did your speech go?"

"In all the excitement, I never wound up making it. I had a bit of an outline by the time we got to Emeryville, then on the bus to Richmond, I thought of a couple good points to make. But as it happened..."

"Probably just as well. They didn't sound like they were amenable to reason anyway. They'd have thrown rotten tomatoes at you by the end."

"I think it worked out well none the less," said Jake. "I'm glad that I went."

"We need to go tomorrow and get you a new cell phone. I suppose that the atheists won't pay for it?"

"They seem strapped for cash, and if the zoning officials in Marin County catch on, they may lose that mansion, as well. So I doubt that they can. And the honorarium they promised is likely to go straight out the window."

"Should we pay back Chi Due for his fuel? The bay area is well outside his normal fishing area."

"I offered, but he said that they found a couple of nests of Ling cod, and apparently it is enough to make his trip a net profit. His men were a bit miffed about taking the body, but he said that they'll get over it. And fortunately, they had enough ice to keep it from being too smelly."

"Nice move, sending it off the island before Rod could dispose of it for good and all. And by the way, what's going to happen to Rod?"

"He'll go to jail, and then he will probably be extradited to the Czech Republic for killing Dr. D."

"Don't they call it Czechia now?"

"I can't bring myself to say it. It's too – I don't know what it is, but it's way too much of it. Anyway, he'll stand trial there for murdering Dobrazamery."

"What was his long term plan? Did he even have one?"

"I think he was so desperate to get out of Europe that he simply seized the first chance he saw. I do wonder, of course, if he'll go to prison here first, or in Europe."

"Does it matter?"

"Well, we were having a good conversation. I wouldn't mind finishing it. I could visit him, maybe."

She laughed. "I hope the State of California can work in a murderer's prison sentence around your convenience," she said.

"If they can't," asked Jake, "Why do we even pay taxes?"

A Party Down in Carthage
By Paolo Gituean*

There's a party down in Carthage, in the old town Punic square;
And all the peeps who don't believe, you know they'll all be there
They'll party through the evening, with their hands up in the air;
And in the morning wake again, in dread and dark despair.

In Rome they sing His praises, the One whose Name they share;
They speak of peace and righteousness and of how the holy fare.
They look for One who'll come back soon, His Name they all declare;
At night they weep for Carthage, and the ones who perish there.

> *"Why must we meet in Carthage,*
> *with blood upon the ground?*
> *Canterbury's neater and a*
> *cleaner, greener town.*
> *Rome is nice this time of year,*
> *and Nashville has its charm;*
> *Why must we meet in Carthage,*
> *where the children come to harm?"*

There's a murder down in Carthage, in the old town Punic square;
And all the peeps who don't believe, they'll say how much they care.
They'll say it breaks the contract, and perhaps they'll even swear;
But when the smoke all clears away, they're really only scared.

If there's murder up in Rome-town, there's panic in the streets;
Any sheep that's shorn up there, he cries aloud and bleats.
In Rome they hope for justice, and the return of stolen fleece;
But they then forgive the shearer as they pray on bended knees.

The Romans work with logic as they try to make their case
Underestimating badly the Resistance that they face.
Punics use derision on foundations made of laughter:
A castle built on circles, and a straw man for its rafters.

Like the Scipios before them for many miles all around
Salt and light the Romans try to sow deep into the ground
But still the Punics fight them and demand they all retreat
Before the Lars Porcena whom they've made for Rome's defeat

There comes a day, the Romans say, when all will be set right
Punics laugh and shake their heads, and party till it's light
All roads lead straight to Carthage, or else to Roman might
All roads must lead to Rome, or else to darkest Punic night.

selah.

This poem is found in Paolo Gituean's *Moldovan Starlight*
© 2024 by Paolo Gituean, a pseudonym
Used by permission

* **EDITOR'S NOTE:** As is common in modern reprints of Gituean's works, the apparent printing errors – the random lines and letters, different in every printing – have been removed from this poem. Purists wishing a more authentic Gituean experience are advised to find older printings.

Geographical Note:

RED ROCK ISLAND DOES exist, and it is located as described, in the San Francisco Bay, off the coast of Richmond, not far from Emeryville. It truly does look like a huge pile of paprika. It is the only privately-owned island in the bay. And it has steep sides and was once mined for manganese.

There, nearly all resemblance with this story stops.

It does not have a flat place near the top to accommodate a house of the size described. The top is also not large enough for the sweeping grassfire scene. There is no abandoned mining site filled with leftover equipment, nor a dock, nor a winding road full of switchbacks going up to the peak.

Accessing the island by any means is likely to be illegal, possibly a tort, and dangerous as well. The cliffs look steep, and the potential for a landslide seems rather high. Building a house there, especially without the knowledge of the legal owners of the island, is inadvisable at best.

If one were to send a Morse code signal to send fescue, it is unlikely that a turf merchant would accommodate your request, though I am told that other sorts of grass might have been delivered and no questions asked. Still, the seed delivery is an unlikely detail. Of course, it's possible that Jake only told that part of the story to amuse Bryly.

Even though the island is privately-owned, it lies with the boundaries of three different counties, making the amount of red tape necessary for plan approval absolutely insane. And that's before we consider either the coastal commission or the two marine conservation districts involved. Had the manganese miners not long ago given up operations, they'd have been shut down by now anyway.

Thus, the house at the top of the hill will never be built, and if it were, there is no way that it would not be obvious from the bridge. The authorities would quickly come calling with questions of code, permits, and general legality. There is also the small matter of the impossibility of supplying utilities to the island in any practical manner, so there would be no water, no power, and no gas. Those last problems could be overcome, if one were willing to live like it's 1899.

The impracticality of the house as described in this story is primarily for the purpose of demonstrating the impracticality of the atheist worldview. It has no practical foundation, and is built very close to the edge of the cliff.

Not to mention, of course, that it fulfills the narrative purpose of providing a place for Jake to be isolated with a group of atheists in the classic murder mystery trope of the isolated group in which there is a killer. That's what I needed, and Red Rock Island fit the bill.

Contrast is the key – hey, wait a minute, I'm just giving you a geographical note here, not deconstructing the entire plot. For goodness sake, just read the story and enjoy it, and don't worry about the impracticalities of the location.

Unless, of course, you're reviewing the book for a major magazine, in which case, we can talk.

A Further Note, on Worldviews:

IT IS INEVITABLE, I suppose, that I will be accused of playing fast and loose with positions and viewpoints. I will be accused of making straw men with atheist positions, or at least of grossly misrepresenting them.

I will confess that Guthrie and Ashton are used more for their comical aspects than their analytics. The others, however, take positions that I have heard expressed to me by actual atheists. For that matter, Guthrie's ploy that Buddhism is only a philosophy (not a true religion *per se*), and that moral obligation comes from an unknown (as yet) law of nature – That is a real position which has been sincerely expressed to me, on at least two occasions.

When Rod says, as he is wont to do, that all roads lead to Rome, or else to Carthage, he is speaking for me. All of my readings in philosophy have brought me to that conclusion. Someone who seeks truth, wherever it take him, will wind up as either a Christian or a nihilist.

The surprising thing for me, when I, as a college freshman, was introduced to Franz Kafka, was that he sounded familiar. I had only read one other existentialist to that time, and then as an exercise in French literature, not as a philosophical study. But they struck the same note, though Camus soft-pedalled it and Kafka beat it like a gong: *It's all absurd. It makes no sense. Life as we know it is just a farce.*

The familiarity of Kafka came from *Ecclesiastes*, a writing by Solomon of Jerusalem, ca. 1000 BC. In it, Solomon describes the utter futility of various fields of endeavor, listing among them the collection of wise sayings. And yet, because of his wise sayings, some claim that Solomon was the wisest of all men. He, too, is expressing the absurdity of it all, but unlike the moderns, he draws a conclusion: Live simply, enjoy life, and serve God.

Once I finally had a name for what I had read in *Ecclesiastes*, I started to see existentialism and its partner, nihilism, in nearly everything I read. The more modern the writer, the more likely it was that he would express the futility and absurdity of life. The more modern the artist, the more likely it was that he would try to express himself through absurd images and utterly incomprehensible abstractions.

For unrelated reasons, I eventually came to my own personal crisis of faith, but I won't go into that here, except to say that I stripped down my assumptions, examined each one, and built back my worldview with only things I could rationally justify. I made two rules, and did my best to apply them pragmatically: That one must believe what is true, however one feels about it; and that one must not discard ideas until one is certain that they are flawed. Knowing where the wisest of the modern philosophers had led us was a part of my analysis.

The ultimate outcome of that whole experience was the observation that sincerely seeking truth, not caring where the search takes one, leads to one of two places, and the difference between them is one single axiom. I nearly became a nihilist then, but didn't.

Years after that crisis of faith, I stumbled onto a book by Tolstoy, *My Confession*. It's a small book, and one of his later works, after he had thrown himself into his role as the Tsar's conscience. I could not put it down.

To my surprise, Tolstoy had come to the same conclusions that I had. He had become a nihilist – some will argue that he was *The Nihilist*, and the paragon of that view – and then had reasoned his way back into the Christian faith, albeit at a very different point from where he started.

It began when he, successful by any reasonable worldly measure, began to awaken with the thoughts, *Why are you here? Is there something you are supposed to be doing? If so, what is it?*

Those questions are the very holy grail of philosophical questions. They demand the one thing nihilism cannot offer: **The Meaning of Life.**

Tolstoy lived in a time when one might be a generalist, and pursue various arts and sciences without being pigeonholed into a single one. And so he did. His largest and most famous works, *War and Peace*, and *Anna Karenina*, had already made him famous, exposing his powerful mind to the world. People flocked to him for wisdom, and he taught them – as he himself later said, he arrogantly taught them things that he, himself, did not know.

None of the sciences could answer his questions, nor could any field of study at all. He found a dichotomy between mental and spiritual studies, which dealt with infinite things (as he called them), and the physical sciences, which taught only of finite things.

There was no study that bridged both. And so he found futile equations that took him nowhere: $A = A$, $X = X$, $0 = 0$. To find a meaning that connected the finite, the observable, the seemingly meaningless physical world to an infinite world where there was true objective meaning, he needed to have elements of both the finite and the infinite in the same equation.

And this brought him back to the church, the one bridge between the finite world and the infinite one. Only there could his questions be answered at last.

Interestingly, in one part of his book, Tolstoy quotes from *Ecclesiastes* repeatedly, drawing parallels to his own findings. The book which tells us that ever possible investment of our time and energy, save one, is like chasing after the wind – that is the book that showed Tolstoy where to turn for meaning.

All of reason, then, seems to lead either to nihilism – one cannot fault Tolstoy for ignorance, nor for a lack of intellectual rigor, nor for a shortage of diligence – or else back to Rome; that is, Christianity.

C.S. Lewis followed this same path, to Carthage and back. He was often accused of reconverting as a psychological wish-fulfillment ploy, to which he would scornfully respond, "Why should a mouse wish for a cat?"

Nothing that I have read since has been able to dissuade me from this belief: *All roads lead to Rome, or else to Carthage.* In the end, we must all either become Christians, with purpose and meaning, or become Punics, living in a labyrinth of random and meaningless chaos.

In this book, which you have just read, only Jake and Rod understand this. The others are stuck between the two: They impose the rules of Rome (such as "Thou shalt not murder") upon lawless Carthage. You will see that pattern often in today's atheists: They will tell you that there can be an objective moral obligation without there being an underlying objective moral truth; that they can subjectively, or by a common belief among a society, or by a social contract, impose moral obligation.

Such people have not followed their philosophies all the way to the end. This realization is how Jake knew that Rod, alone, of all those present, could have murdered Ulysses. Their points of view are separated by one axiom, but it is a big one: Rod believes that God does not exist, and lives like it. Jake, in contrast, believes that God does exist, and lives like it.

Perhaps this book will spark some thinking. I've tried hard to avoid pounding the pulpit. In the end, if a few readers get off the fence and move into one of the two camps, then my work is done. And if none move, then no harm has been done.

But would I really wish to move an atheist fully to nihilism? Yes, I think I would: From there, he, like Tolstoy, can find the one bridge that unites the finite and the infinite. There, he, like Solomon, can perhaps realize that the other end of the road has meaning that can come from no other earthly pursuit.

There I'll leave it, Friends. Agree with me, disagree with me, enjoy the story but not the ideas, or enjoy the ideas but not the plot. In the words of Pontius Pilate:

Quod Scripsi, Scripsi.

www.ingramcontent.com/pod-product-compliance
Lightning Source LLC
Chambersburg PA
CBHW020642250626
47154CB00008B/2780